ready or not

SPECIAL EDITION

JENN PLUMMER

WildLupine BOOKS

join jenn plummer's readers' group

Stay up to date with Jenn Plummer by joining her Facebook readers' group, Jenn's Harlots. Ask questions, get first looks at new books/series, and have fun with other book lovers!

https://www.facebook.com/groups/jennsharlots/

a note from the author

Dear readers,

Ready or Not takes place within the Aspen Ridge universe and may contain minor spoilers of other books. Unlike the full-length novels, this novella is a dark romance. There is no cheating (between MCs), no sharing, both adults are always willing participants (even if it seems like they aren't), and there is a true HEA.

Themes include dark obsessive stalking, possessive/obsessive MMC, manipulation, explicit language, religion, and sexually explicit content that includes: age gap, dub-con, daddy kink, primal play, knife play, blood play, sadism/masochism, breath play, and somnophilia.

Please read responsibly. If you have any questions about this list please don't hesitate to reach out to the author directly.

Sending you all love.

playlist

Sweet Dreams - Trinix
Nasty - Tinashe
Closer - Nine Inch Nails
Control - Puddle of Mudd
For Your Entertainment - Adam Lambert
Disturbia - Rihanna
Young God - Halsey
Teeth - Lady Gaga
S&M - Rihanna

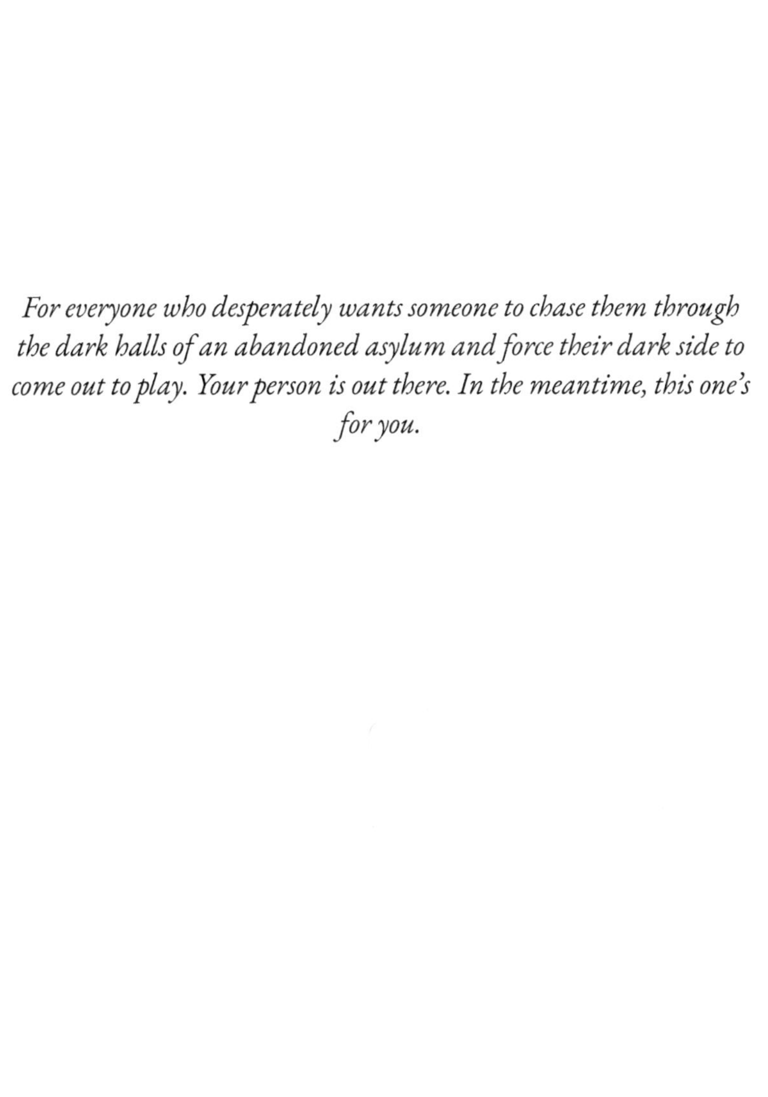

For everyone who desperately wants someone to chase them through the dark halls of an abandoned asylum and force their dark side to come out to play. Your person is out there. In the meantime, this one's for you.

CHAPTER 1

WES

THE HUSTLE AND BUSTLE INSIDE BEAN HAVEN THIS morning makes me groan with irritation. The arrival of fall means that everyone is desperate for one of Hannah Haven's signature pumpkin spice lattes. In hindsight, I should have just brewed some at home, but like everyone else in this town, I was craving Bean Haven coffee. Except I just appreciate a good dark roast coffee, not this flavored seasonal bullshit everyone's currently in line for. It figures that the day a random craving for their coffee hits me falls on the one day a year everyone comes out in droves. I never want to be out in town, much preferring the quiet comfort of my home, and I paid my dues to be able to work in solitude. But this morning, a dire pull to the local shop consumed me, wanting a coffee like I'd lose my mind if I didn't have it.

While checking my email on my phone, the person behind bumps into me, and it takes a massive amount of effort not to let my frustration out on them.

"I'm so sorry, excuse me. That's my fault." Her sweet, cheery voice is music to my ears, an enchanting melody made just for me, and my morning suddenly improves. Realization sets in, and the owner of that voice has my body heating and my dick perking up in my pants. Maybe it wasn't the coffee calling me to Bean Haven after all.

Lilith Aspen.

Daughter of the Aspen family, descendant of the founders of our small Pacific Northwest town, and my twenty-year-old dipshit son's girlfriend. Who also happens to be the most intoxicating woman I've ever seen in my thirty-eight years on Earth.

"Oh, hi, Mr. Draven. Sorry to bump into you like that, everyone seems anxious to get a latte."

"Lilith. It's good to see you. I've told you, it's Wes. I'm not old enough to be a Mr. At least it doesn't feel like it."

She smiles up at me, her sparkling hazel eyes so beautiful and bright, more gold than green or blue, the center a deep brown—dark and forbidden. Just like her. I'm utterly enraptured by her, unable to tear myself away even if I wanted to. She shifts on her feet as I clear my throat.

"You in line for one?" I question.

"A pumpkin spice latte? Guilty. I love pumpkin. Everything about this time of year I'm on board with," she replies, her voice like a siren's call just for me.

"You like fall, huh?" I ask, enjoying this one-on-one conversation more than I should. She tucks a piece of hair behind her ear, her diamond earring catching the light above us—no doubt a gift from her elitist parents. My eyes track the movement as her hand drags down the length of her hair, brushing over her chest before dropping to her side. I slowly bring my eyes forward, back to meet hers, and she smiles adoringly at me. She's too sweet, too good for this fucked up world. But I can't help the call I feel to dirty her up. I'm good at reading people, and something tells me this saccharine facade is a projection she puts on for the outside world. That inside, she's just like me. Dark. All she really wants is to be herself, but can't for whatever reason. Presumably, it has everything to do with where she came from.

"Not so much fall, but all the dark, wickedness of everything in October. It's my favorite month. It's chilly, the leaves are starting to shed all of their gorgeous red, yellow, and orange leaves, the nights are clear, and I can't help but love all the spookiness. You know, some say that my ancestors built Aspen Ridge on top of a burial ground. Might explain all the haunting stories."

Yeah, she's different from what she's putting out there for everyone else. The line moves us forward into the building and I hold the door open for her, placing my hand on her back to usher her in front of me. The heat from inside Bean Haven blasts us and her face flushes, pinkening her fair skin even further.

"So, not a Christmas girl then?"

"No," she laughs. "Absolutely not. Too much of a religious holiday for me and—oh, I'm sorry, that was rude of me, considering . . ."

My eyebrows raise in question, already knowing where she's going with this but wanting to hear it anyway. "Considering?"

"I just assumed that Adam was connected so deeply with his faith because of his parents. Is that not correct?"

I laugh lightly at her assumption, which couldn't have been farther from accurate. Adam's mother and I had him when we were both teenagers. After his birth, she became deeply religious, finding her faith in God and all that glorious jazz. Add that to being two teenagers trying to figure out how to be parents when we still had growing up to do ourselves. It was a recipe for disaster. Luckily, we'd been able to work out a solid co-parenting plan so we were both involved in raising him, while not being in a relationship with each other. Adam just happened to take after his darling mother.

"No, Lilith. He gets that from his mother. I have no faith. Spiritual in my own way, but no, my beliefs are far from Adam's," I chuckle.

If possible, the pink on her cheeks deepens further, turning a deep crimson, most likely in embarrassment. It thrills me, and I wonder what else I could do to her to see that color again.

"I don't mean to laugh, it's reasonable to assume that. Adam and I just aren't close anymore, he very much prefers his mother to me. I assume that's where you two hang out? I haven't seen you with him in a bit."

And I've been waiting for an excuse to see you again.

"Ahh. Well, actually, no." It's her turn to laugh uncomfortably. I turn to face her, my attention solely on her, the noise of everything around us quieting to barely a whisper. "He broke up with me. A few weeks ago."

I can't help the shocked expression on my face, and she laughs again. My son's a fucking idiot. He had this perfect woman and broke up with her? A better man and father would have a talk with him to put some sense into his stupid brain, but I feel like I was just given a gift straight from whatever powers that be. I school my features the best I can, but I know she saw my shocked horror morph into relief and delight.

"I'm sorry to hear that. Are you alright?"

"I'm completely fine. Honestly."

More relief floods my veins.

The line moves forward as we stand together in comfortable silence. I don't fight the urge to roam over her body with my eyes. She's the epitome of perfection. Everything about her calls to the primal, darker side of me. Selfishly, I breathe in deeply, inhaling her scent into my lungs. She smells earthy—dark floral and sage, almost like she walked through incense instead of using perfume. It's rich and sweet, and my mouth waters. Her hair is midnight black, with rich auburn highlights throughout, and hangs to the middle of her back. My hands itch at my sides, begging to reach out and touch her. Any part of her will do. I want to feel the smoothness of her skin on mine. I want to taste her. Hear her siren voice on repeat. I suddenly need to know everything about her. *Everything.*

We finally reach the register where Hannah, Harlow, and Hailey Haven are working the counter to hustle the entire damn town of Aspen Ridge through their coffee shop.

"Good morning! Your usual?" Hannah asks me.

"Yes, please, plus a pumpkin spice latte and . . ." I gesture to the pastry display case next to us. "Anything to eat, Lilith?"

"Oh, uhm, just the latte please."

"Just the two, Hannah. Happy to have your sisters home for some much-needed help?"

"Oh, yes! I needed it today. It would have taken me all day to serve everyone. Hey, Lily!"

"Hey, Hannah, I can't believe how busy you are today!"

"It's wild, but I'm so thankful for the business."

Her sisters are quick to whip up our drinks, and I pull out my card to pay as Lilith digs through her purse. Using this as my excuse to finally reach out and touch her bare skin, I place my hand over hers, stopping her from pulling out her wallet. Electricity zaps through my palm on contact, and her eyes go wide, bouncing back and forth between mine, searching for answers. She felt it too.

"Let me get it. As a thank you for enduring this line with me this morning."

She smiles, and it's the most beautiful thing I've ever seen. Fuck, how I want to take those lips between my teeth. Releasing her hand before I'm ready to, I focus on paying Hannah for our drinks and guide Lilith out of Bean Haven. Once we're outside on the cobblestone sidewalk, she turns to face me, pulling her coat closer to her neck, covering that bit of flesh I want to devour.

"Thank you again, Mr. Draven."

"C'mon, really with the 'Mr. Draven?' I'm thirty-eight, not fifty-eight."

She laughs, and I can't help the smile I give her in return. She's just so breathtaking and enchanting.

"Fine. Thank you for the latte, Wes."

"You're welcome, Lilith. I'll be seeing you."

Sooner than you realize.

"I ran into Lilith today. What happened between you two?" I ask my son over dinner. While Adam lives full-time with his mother now, he comes over once a week for a meal and some forced father-son time. Not that he actually wants to be here. In fact, he typically bails as often as he can, always with some excuse as to why he can't have a simple meal with the man who created him and wants to spend time with him.

"Her name's Lily, I don't know why you call her that, it's weird. And I doubt you want to know why I broke up with her."

Curiosity more than piqued at this point, I give him a look that says *try me*.

"Alright, Dad, you asked for it," he says before taking a deep breath, "she said she understood my desire to abstain from sex until marriage, so we ended up doing some other stuff, once, and not intercourse. But she asked me to give it to her rough. Like rough, rough. Degradation and shit. There's something dark about her. I don't like it." Adam looks truly tortured and horrified, and if I wasn't having a conversation with my son, my cock would be waking up, eager to take the job over. I wasn't expecting that turn of events, or to gain that knowledge about what sweet, little Lilith Aspen likes in the bedroom. Even if it confirms my theory about her. Clearing my throat, I keep my composure firmly in place.

"And you're not into that?" I ask, knowing full well his mother's influence has made him the devout Christian he is. He has a set of deeply rooted values that he lives by.

"Definitely, not. I thought Lily was a good girl. Her parents told Mom that she was angelic, like the kind of girl you want to bring home to your parents and marry someday. I don't want a wife with that kind of appetite. Her parents clearly have no idea they raised a temptress."

I give him another look before speaking.

"So, this has everything to do with your faith?"

"That, too. Prayed on it good and hard, and *Lilith* isn't right for me. She'll find someone for her but it won't be me. I'm sure it'll be someone equally messed up."

"Everyone has to do what's best for them, aren't you supposed to 'not cast judgment?'" I ask.

"I can judge because it affected me. You've said that before. Breaking up with a potential whore for a wife was definitely the right decision."

My immediate reaction comes on quickly and unrestrained. My fists ball at my sides and my jaw ticks before I speak through clenched teeth.

"Watch your damn mouth, Adam. Don't call her that again."

"For real? Why do you care if I call her a whore? Only whores want to be treated that way. Would you rather me call her a harlot?"

"Did you not hear what I just said?" My voice raises, leaving no room for misunderstanding.

"Loud and clear, Dad. Whatever. I'm heading home. I'll talk to you later, I guess."

Adam slings his bag over his shoulder and walks out, the door slamming behind him. Really fucking holy of him to call someone expressing their sexuality in a safe space a whore. Fuck, I hope he didn't call her that to her face.

Letting my irritation with my idiot son go, I grab my laptop to spiral down a rabbit hole and gain access to some information. It's what I do best.

I went to college for cybersecurity, earned several industry certifications, and found my niche when I became extremely good at hacking. I got a certification in penetration testing, and after causing some waves on the dark web, I was picked up by a private security company as a member of their red team. Then I went solo and got my license to be a private investigator. I work for clients all over the state of Washington, and a bit farther into other Pacific Northwest states if needed. Since everyone's electronic footprint is so large nowadays, I'm overloaded with information, ready to dig up whatever someone might need.

The money I made while working in private security put me in a nice little spot to settle down and be picky about the jobs I take. The last one was actually right here in Aspen Ridge. The owner of Aspen Ridge Distillery, Sawyer Hayes, hired me to track his girl's stalker ex-boyfriend. Luckily, I got to the bottom of his shitty-ass plans before too much damage was done. Props to Sawyer for hiring me and not giving a damn about what boundaries he had to cross to protect what's his. I'd do the same if my woman was harmed or her life was in jeopardy. Who wouldn't?

I get comfortable in my seat, settling in for a long night. Time to find out everything I can about Lilith Aspen.

I log in to my computer to do what I do best.

Hunt.

lily

THE WEEK LEADING UP TO HALLOWEEN IS ALWAYS bittersweet. Like every year, eagerness for the town's festivities fills me, but with it comes a lingering bitterness that my favorite holiday is almost over again. My family hosts a harvest festival every year, and the entire town shuts down for it. Downtown Aspen Ridge gets transformed into what October dreams are made of. Tents with games and activities, a hay bale maze, booths for local businesses, and more pumpkin and apple themed food and drinks than you could possibly want.

But what I really can't wait for? The costume party on Halloween night at the old, abandoned asylum, deep in the woods of Aspen Ridge. The building, originally called Western Washington Asylum for the Chronically Insane, sits at the base of the Olympic National Forest, hidden amongst the lush rainforest, surrounded by mountains and massive trees. First built in the 1800s, the stories of the atrocities that went on behind closed doors are well known, and it's said that the souls still haunt it today. The asylum closed its doors in the 1970s. Everything was left exactly as it was when it was in operation, frozen in time and pillaged over the years. Now, every year on Halloween night, there is a party in the crumbling shell of what used to be. While it's frowned upon, no one has outright shut it down yet.

Per usual, I find myself waiting outside an old brick building on Main Street for my best friend, Emma. She's notoriously late and lucky I love her as much as I do. To kill time while I wait for her, I lean up against the side of the building and pull out my phone. At least we don't have lunch reservations. Barrel House, the only real restaurant option in Aspen Ridge, is usually pretty quick to have seating at lunchtime. Lost in my own world, my skin suddenly prickles with goosebumps. The hair on my arms stands up and a cold trickle tingles down my spine. I look up from my phone and scan the area. Everyone who is out is in their own little world, but I can't help feeling like I'm being watched. It's probably Emma messing with me. My eyes go back to my phone when it vibrates in my hand with an incoming text message.

Unknown: It was good to see you the other day. I just wanted to check on you.

Who the hell?

Me: Sorry, who is this?

The reply comes immediately. Three little bubbles pop up and my heart dips into my stomach when the words appear.

Unknown: Wes.

. . .

Wes Draven. The hottest dad-I'd-like-to-fuck I've ever met in my twenty years of life. Quickly changing his name in my contacts, I reply, a smile that I can't control on my face the entire time.

> Me: It was good to run into you too. I'm great, honestly. Why wouldn't I be?

D.I.L.F: The breakup?

> Me: No offense because he's your son, but my feelings aren't hurt. I know my worth, Mr. Draven, I'm better off. Someday, someone will see me and give me what I need.

D.I.L.F: That's a very mature way to look at things. You're not what I expected.

I chuckle at that. He has no idea. I've struggled to relate to other girls my age because of our vast maturity level differences. Emma is the exception, and I'm so thankful for her. I'd much rather have one real, life-long best friend than a whole gang of fakes pretending to be in my corner. Adam breaking up with me did me a favor. After our last conversation, I would have broken up with him if he hadn't in the heat of the moment.

> Me: I hope that's a compliment

D.I.L.F: It is.

> Me: That all you wanted, Mr. Draven? To check on me?

D.I.L.F: Not even a little bit, Lilith

My cheeks flame in a blush. Is he flirting with me? Before I can formulate a reply, Emma walks up and breaks the spell.

"Who's got my best friend blushing like that? Please tell me you aren't talking to Father Adam."

The laugh that bursts from me is loud and obnoxious, as it always is when we're together.

"How many times do I have to tell you not to call him that?" I slap her arm before leaning in to give her a hug.

"You two aren't together anymore, any name that was previously off-limits is now firmly back in the have-at-it category. But seriously, who are you talking to all flustered? Spill it. I've got nothing but time, and I'm craving a harvest apple cider margarita."

"That sounds disgusting. I love apples and tequila, but the two don't mix, Em."

"Maybe you're just jealous that you're not twenty-one yet and can't have one, hmm?"

"You're annoying."

We walk down the stone steps on the side of the building that leads to the door of Barrel House. For being a small town in the Pacific Northwest, they really know how to keep things fresh. Barrel House is gorgeously decorated with a speakeasy vibe that I'm obsessed with. We're seated right away, and as we follow the hostess, the chilling feeling of being watched returns. I look around again, but don't find anyone openly watching me or even looking in my direction. Maybe the veil has thinned enough and the ghosts of Aspen Ridge have come out to play.

Taking our seats in one of the emerald-tufted booths, I strip my coat off and brace myself for Emma's inability to let anything go. Deciding to get ahead of her questions, I give her what she wants.

"So, I wasn't texting with 'Father Adam,' more like Adam's *father...*"

I await the lashing of rapid-fire questions, but instead, I get a dirty, mischievous smirk. Her face lit up like a Christmas tree.

"And what did Mr. Hot-as-fuck have to say?"

Relieved that she's not weirded out or disappointed that I'm this worked up over a man nearly twenty years older than me, not to mention my ex's dad, I relax fully. I should have known better. Emma is the least judgmental person I've ever met. She's so open and free-spirited.

"Okay, so it's not just me then? He's soooo hot, Em. Why is he so hot?"

"Girl, I don't know, but I would climb him like a tree if given the chance. Those muscles, those forearms covered in tattoos. Mmm, mmm. Mmm!" She sinks into the booth like she's melting, and I laugh at her, but she's not wrong. She's actually extremely spot on.

"Definitely the tattoos, especially on his hands. And that beard. Jesus." I fan my face, which I know is heating again in a flushed tint.

"So, what did he want?"

"We ran into each other the other day at Bean Haven, and I told him Adam had broken up with me."

"You didn't tell him why?"

"Ha! No. I doubt he wants to hear that I asked his son to fuck my face. God, Emma!"

"Hey, maybe he'd do it. He looks like he knows all sorts of things."

"Right? One can only wish."

If I'm being honest with myself, I do wish. From the moment I first met Wes, there was something about him that called to me. I may have suggested we hang out at Adam's dad's house on more than one occasion just so I could catch a glimpse of him. Sure, he's gorgeous in a mysterious, taboo kind of way, but there's something darker about him that intrigues me. I want to peel back all of his layers and see the depth underneath. Accepting my rightful place in hell, where Adam told me I'd be headed, I'm okay with admitting that I've touched myself to thoughts of him too many times to count. He's a deliciously dark fantasy that I'll have on repeat for as long as I can, as taboo as that is. Who has frequent sex dreams about their—now ex—boyfriend's dad?

I've always been a ridiculously deep sleeper, never dreaming or waking even if a hurricane took the house down. But lately, my fantasies are so vivid, so real, that when I wake up, it's almost disorienting. And they're always filled with Wes Draven.

The waiter comes over and takes our orders, potato and leek soup with French bread for me, and a club sandwich for Emma, paired with her harvest apple margarita.

"So, how's the new job?" I ask, curious to know what it's like to work at a boxing gym.

"It's been good. Pretty easy to learn the ropes. Honestly, it took me the longest to get used to the smell. Sweat lingers, babe, and it's not cute."

I throw my head back in a laugh. That sounds like hell to me. Even though her view of sexy, half-naked men is something to be jealous of. Last week she started working at Knockout, the only gym in Aspen Ridge. While it has your typical gym equipment, it mainly caters to boxing, muay Thai, Krav Maga, and self-defense. The owner, Dominic, is hot as sin. Not to mention, it's no secret the Hayes brothers frequently box each other there, and those men are a different breed of gorgeous.

"I bet the view isn't bad though," I say as I give her a cheeky smile, wiggling my eyebrows.

"Girl, you have no idea. One in particular makes me lose all my focus, and I turn into a puddle. I'm surprised he even hired me as a receptionist. Even if it is part-time."

"Oh my god, do you mean, Dom? I swear I thought you were going to say one of the Hayes, or even Reid-freaking-Knight."

"Nope," she says, popping the 'p'.

"Daaaaaamn. Are you going after him?"

"Fuck no. I need this job. Sleeping with your boss is sure to make things messy. No thank you, sir. I'll happily ogle the shit out of him safely behind my desk, him and his two best friends."

Our food arrives, and we eat and have the kind of conversation that flows easily between two women who've been close their entire lives. Before we know it, lunch service has ended and the staff is preparing for dinner service. By the time we get outside, the sun is setting. The way we lose track of time when it's just the two of us is the reason we don't make any other plans when we're together. A simple lunch date can easily bleed into the late evening. Emma and I say our goodbyes and head in opposite directions.

I pull my coat closer to my body as the autumn air blows through our mountain town. The sky was overcast today but as the moon came out, the clouds cleared, giving a warm glow to light my way as I walk through downtown to my apartment, the crisp leaves rustling and crunching under my feet. As the wind blows lightly again, a shiver runs down my spine and a haunting, eerie sensation creeps over me. I come to a stop on the cobblestone sidewalk and look around but no one's there. The strange feeling that someone is lurking in the shadows, their presence following me like a ghost I can't quite shake, surrounds me. I quicken my pace, walking briskly by the various shops that fill our town center, every step echoing into the silent night. The wind blows again, and the light from the moon casts shadows that move across the ground and climb the sides of the old brick buildings, amplifying the eerie sensation enveloping me.

Despite the unsettling feeling, thrill courses through my veins, and I can't hold back a smile. I could only be so lucky to have a ghost haunt me. The closer I get to the edge of town, the darkness seems to deepen, that sinister feeling holding me hostage, sending goosebumps across my skin and a chill down my spine. Once I reach my small apartment at the very end of Main Street, sitting off on its own, I look around once more, convinced there is someone watching me.

Or hunting me.

The unnerving sensation of being watched grips me once again as I step out of the bathroom. Clutching my towel tightly around me, the chilling droplets from my wet hair against my back send shivers rippling across my skin. Looking around my room, I'm paralyzed by the sight of a deep crimson rose resting on my pillow. Moving quickly through my apartment, inspecting closets and looking under the bed, I search for the phantom that was here and find everything completely undisturbed. The flood of disappointment should concern me.

Returning to my bed, I pick up the rose, a thorn nicking the pad of my thumb. Wincing, I suck on my wounded finger, the taste of iron exploding on my tongue. Carefully holding the rose again, I admire the delicate petals, the wilting of the edges, and the soft, velvety texture. My heart races in my chest, a pulsing sensation growing deep within me, my breaths coming in erratic bursts. This shouldn't turn me on. Someone was in my room. There's no ghost following me. It's someone very real. I want to admonish myself for the reaction I'm having, the excitement and thrill of the temptation of something much, much darker than I've ever experienced. I should be recoiling from the potential danger, but there's something so sweet when fear mixes with arousal.

Walking to the window that faces the miles of woods behind my apartment, I look out into the dark expanse of the landscape. With the only light coming from the moon, I couldn't see someone if I wanted to. Instead, the feeling rises, convincing me that someone is out there staring back at me. I *know* someone is watching me, and it speaks directly to the part of me I keep buried.

Feeling impulsive and slightly crazed, I let the towel go, allowing it to fall from my body and pool at my feet, putting my entire naked body on display. Holding the rose between my fingers, I drag the soft bud down, across my neck, letting it trail lightly over my skin, across my chest, and between my breasts. The soft petals send waves of goosebumps across my sensitive flesh as it reaches my stomach. I let the rose fall from my fingers and flutter to the ground, moving my hands to grasp my breasts, caressing them in my palms before pinching the stiff peaks of my nipples hard between two fingers. Working them over, my hips start to gyrate of their own accord, my empty pussy clenching and unclenching, begging to be filled with something, anything.

A needy whimper releases from my lips and I give in, putting two fingers into my mouth to soak them before using my other hand to spread open my pussy. I drag those damp fingers through my center, gathering up the wetness pooled between my legs and pressing them to my throbbing clit. My head drops to the side as the sensations pulse through my body. I'm liquid fire, rocking my hips back and forth over my hand, my fingers rubbing circles across the silky nub that makes me feel so damn good. The pleasure comes quickly, the idea that someone is out there watching me, fueling my desire. I hope he got off to it, I hope whoever is out there has his cock out, beating off to watching me touch myself. My orgasm spreads through my body, my knees trembling, mouth falling slightly ajar. When I'm too sensitive to touch, I wipe through my slick center and drag my fingers down the pane of the window, leaving behind the essence of my pleasure for whoever is out there.

And I know they are there.

CHAPTER 3

WES

I KNEW LUSTING AFTER MY SON'S GIRLFRIEND WAS wrong, but fuck if I could help it. Not that I tried hard to fight my desire. Lilith was everything. From the moment he brought her home I was knocked off-kilter. She became the center of my gravity and didn't even know it. My obsession. The way I yearned to see her, even if it was just a glimpse, made my heart race in anticipation, to the point of pain. I wanted to be engulfed in her presence, to drown in her. Every passing second away from her felt like an eternity. Now that I know she's single, watching Lilith has become my addiction.

I know she feels me, always close by but never making myself known. I know it's wrong, but I can't control it. I don't want to. I won't fight it because I'm too far gone for her. That little show she gave me last night at her window sealed her fate. There's a filthy side to her that she's aware of, she's just had to keep it hidden for so long. I need to free her; that side she keeps locked up tight. Which is how I ended up sitting in the window seat of Bean Haven drinking a hot coffee while watching her help decorate Main Street for the Aspen family's annual harvest festival.

Following her yesterday was exquisite. I love how intuitive she is, how she responds is so beautiful. Her body language changes, becoming more alert; her facial expressions showing fear and curiosity, even temptation. She feels me close by. Every time my eyes are on her she picks up on it immediately, and her spine stiffens as she looks around for her admirer. She's always left disappointed though, I won't make myself known until I'm ready to claim her.

Today Lilith is wearing a pair of black leggings that hug every lithe inch of her legs, a large, slouchy maroon sweater, brown boots that stop right under her knee, and a pair of cream socks that stick out the top. She's cute as fuck with her hair tied up in a bun, and big gold hoop earrings. I flip through the photos on my laptop that I've taken of her over the last week, and my dick stirs to life, ready to claim what's his. I keep an eye on Lilith while sifting through the information I've gathered. I've made a good living out of being a private investigator, so following her and gaining access to all the information I could ever want was child's play.

A lot of it I already knew based on her last name, everyone in AR is familiar with the Aspens. The family name has been commonplace since they founded the town and named it after themselves.

After going over her background for the hundredth time, I lose myself to hacking into her social media accounts, which was easier than it should have been, and I plan to talk to her about creating secure passwords. While I'm busy scrolling through her photos and reading her messages, I find a little golden ticket. Marcus Chamberlin wants to take my little one on a date—no doubt per his parents' request—and suggested driving into the city for a nice meal on the water and getting a hotel room after. Pretentious fuck. She doesn't need your money and a charming dinner at a steakhouse, she needs to be held down by her throat and devoured like the goddess she is.

Lilith suggests they go to the Halloween party at the old abandoned asylum instead, and it fills me with excitement and pride.

And just like that, my girl paved the way for me to finally take what's mine.

Lost to planning exactly how I want Halloween night to go, while also keeping my eyes on her as she helps spread faux spider-webs across the window pane of Book Bound, I don't notice when my son walks in with his arm slung over a girl's shoulders. They walk through Bean Haven and get in line, ordering their seasonal drinks before Adam even realizes I'm sitting here.

"Oh, hey, Dad."

The young girl under his arm awkwardly walks forward with him, her arm around his lower back and her other holding a mug of, what's no doubt, steaming hot pumpkin garbage.

"Hey, Adam."

"You working from here? Weird seeing you out of the house. Oooh wait, are you on assignment? Who's the mark?"

I ignore his ignorant comments, he knows the rules and shouldn't be talking about what I do in front of anyone, and especially not outside of the house, in case I am currently on assignment. But I want to know who the girl is.

"Are you going to introduce me to your date or just continue to be rude?" I ask him, appalled. I thought I taught him better than this. What did Lilith ever see in him?

As if I summoned her, in she walks, her eyes immediately connecting with mine. She holds them for a moment before looking away, and I helplessly watch the moment she sees Adam and the girl he has already moved on with. She looks them both up and down before rolling her eyes and walking to the counter to place her order—no doubt a pumpkin spice latte.

"Hi, sir, I'm Eden. I'm not from here. We met at a mission program through our churches. It's so nice to finally meet you."

Finally? My idiot son either moves on quickly or there's some concerning overlap here.

Out of the corner of my eye, I watch Lilith take her to-go cup and pastry bag from Hannah before walking our way, chin lifted, shoulders held back, and spine straight. That's my girl. Show him what he's missing. I bet if I spread her out on the table right now and ate her pussy until she screamed my name, he'd really realize exactly what he's missing. Not that he'll ever get a chance with her again. She's mine.

"Hey, Mr. Draven, Adam. Who's this?" she says, her head cocking to the side as she pulls out a chair and sits across from me. Her confidence, whether false bravado or not, is attractive as fuck. Yes, little girl, make waves, come alive for daddy.

Adam shifts on his feet and looks around blankly as he stumbles over how to answer. Eden puts out her hand in Lilith's direction to offer a handshake as she speaks, "I'm Eden, Adam's girlfriend."

To my surprise, Lilith doesn't feign shock, irritation, or anger. She smiles brightly, condescendingly, and I seem to be the only one aware of it. Did she already know?

"That's so cute! How long have you two been . . . what do you call it? Dating? Courting?"

"Courting. And—"

"We really need to be heading out," Adam interrupts as he tries to steer Eden away from the fun.

"No, son, I insist. I'd love to know what's going on in your life. How long has this been a thing, Eden? Go on."

"Oh, six months or so. Time has been flying, but we're so in love. Isn't that right, Adam?" she says as she looks up at my moron spawn with doe eyes, oblivious to the fact that he was two-timing her."

"Ahh, must explain why he didn't want to put his cock in me. I thought it was because something was wrong with it but clearly, he was too busy putting it in you."

By some miracle, I keep my features under control as I pick up my coffee and take a slow sip, hiding my smirk. I've said it before, my son is a goddamn idiot. Lilith gives both of them a huge smile while Eden's mouth hangs open like a trout, her face bright red in embarrassment, or horror. Probably a decent mix of both. Adam looks equally stunned, as if he didn't expect Lilith to be so crude. He doesn't know my girl.

"I'll meet you outside, Eden, she's a liar and out of her mind. I'll be right there."

Eden listens to him, not surprisingly. I'm sure being raised to be a subservient little housewife and bear lots of children has taught her to obey him well. Adam's face morphs the moment the bell chimes above the door, signaling Eden's departure, and I sit up straighter, no longer relaxed and amused. His eyebrows pinch together as he leans against his hand on the table, bending forward into Lilith's space.

"You know why I didn't fuck you, Lily, I didn't lie about waiting until marriage." The words are forced, his molars grinding together. "But there's something evil about you. There's darkness there, and I wouldn't take a chance with you if you were the last woman on Earth. Only the devil himself would want you."

"Well, Adam, thank god for that! Fingers crossed he finds me. Sounds like he'd be a good time. Real godly of you to cheat, by the way. But I heard your God forgives, so lucky you."

"Adam, I think you're done here." My voice is firm, leaving no room for argument. I've had enough of this shitshow, and I'm ready to talk to Lilith alone.

"Yeah, you're right. I don't want to spend any more time in the presence of such filth."

"Adam," I growl. He looks at me before looking back at Lilith and I stand abruptly, moving to get out of the booth. Lucky for Adam, he gets the hint and leaves, walking out the door and leaving me alone in the booth with Lilith. Settling back into my seat, I take her in, trying to get a read on how she's feeling. Her face is tilted down toward her coffee, her long, manicured nails rapping across the top of the table, as she's lost in thought. I reach forward hesitantly, placing my hand over hers in hopes of offering her support. When she looks up, her eyes are unreadable as they flick down to where our hands are connected. Disappointment flows through me as she slowly pulls them free into her lap . I have the strongest desire to comfort her, to erase all memories of anyone who came before me.

"I'm fine, Mr. Draven. And also mortified. I'm so sorry you had to hear all of that. I kind of saw red and just reacted."

"It's Wes. There's nothing to be mortified about. Dad or not, I'm still human, and you defended yourself, you should be proud of that."

"Still. I'm sure you could have lived a loooong happy life without hearing those details."

"Trust me, Lilith, knowing those things only makes me see what an idiot my son is. He didn't realize what he had right in front of him."

"You mean a dark, evil demon?"

I look into her beautiful hazel eyes, captivated by the power she has over me; the darkness that plays in her irises, the secrets locked behind them, drawing me in like a moth to a flame. She pulls me deeper and deeper with each passing moment. I don't look away when I answer her question.

"Yes."

Her plump pink lips turn up, eyes squinting with malice and mischief, and my heart nearly bursts in my chest. She has no fucking idea who she really is, who she could be if she just gave in to the dark desires simmering just below the surface of those bewitching eyes. Soon enough, I'm going to show her.

There's no going back now.

CHAPTER 4

lily

The night of the harvest festival is finally here, and downtown Aspen Ridge has been transformed into a spooky, Gothic wonderland, ready for people to traipse through. I spent the entire day helping decorate with the volunteers my parents recruited, and the whole time I couldn't shake that now-familiar uneasy sensation that prickled at the back of my neck and down my spine. The feeling that eyes were on me everywhere I went, that someone was lurking in the shadows, biding their time. It was a heady feeling, to be the center of someone's attention but not be able to identify who. I tried to ignore the thrill that rushed through me when I gave it thought, willing them to show themselves. I threw myself into the busywork, helping where I was needed, but that inexplicable chill stayed with me, an ominous presence haunting me.

I get dressed in my favorite pair of denim jeans with cuffed bottoms and pair them with brown booties, a cream sweater, and my favorite black pleather jacket, knowing I'll only get a few more wears out of it before winter arrives in AR. I feel confident. After having my hair pulled back all day, I washed and styled it in big loose waves, and put on a light layer of makeup. I warred with whether or not to rock my favorite red lipstick but decided to go for it. I feel as close to the real me as I dare get and ready for one of my favorite nights leading up to Halloween.

I stroll down the street by myself, the chilly autumn wind whispering over the cobblestone sidewalk, swirling fallen leaves and making them dance around like long-forgotten ghosts of the souls here before us. Flickering lanterns hang from posts along both sides of the street, casting twisted shadows that seem to reach out to every passerby.

I weave through the heavily decorated street, making my way through the maze of vendor stalls, taking my time to admire each. Now that the sun has set, Downtown Aspen Ridge truly feels like a fall fantasyland. The air is thick with the smell of cinnamon and bonfire, and I inhale it deeply into my lungs, following it like the call of a siren. An unsettling chill wraps around me, and I pull my jacket tighter around my body, adjusting my scarf as I walk in search of the origin of the most amazing, mouthwatering scent. The wind blows again, my heart skipping in my chest in anticipation of something ominous, goosebumps scattering across my covered arms.

Am I losing my mind to madness? The only thing keeping me from losing my grasp on reality is the rose. I'm not being haunted, I'm being hunted. Suddenly, that strange feeling of being watched is back in full force and I turn quickly, looking around to see who it could be. As soon as I spin on the heels of my boots, I run face-first into a hard chest.

"Oomph! I'm so sorry!"

Two large, tattooed hands jut out, grabbing me around both arms to hold me steady, but instead of pushing me away, I'm pulled in. The smell of fresh soap, cedar, and something warm and spicy fills my nose, calming my racing heart.

"We've got to stop meeting like this." The deep, sexy voice cascades over me like a warm, welcoming caress, waking my entire body.

"Mr. Draven. Sorry to bump into you again," I say, trying to right myself from his arms.

"I didn't say I was complaining, Lilith," he whispers as his eyes roam over my body. Even though it's hidden by my coat and clothes, it feels as though I'm standing exposed, naked in front of him, and based on his expression, he's picturing just that. My cheeks redden, warming as my body heats from the inside out. It's hard not to bask under his attention. He's so gorgeous and looks at me like I'm the only one around.

"You here with anyone?" I ask, curious if he's seeing anyone, not that I could act on these depraved fantasies. Since leaving Bean Haven the other day, I haven't been able to shake him from my thoughts. Wes looks at me like he sees me. The real me, stripped bare in my rawest, most pure form, and there's no judgment, only pride and what looks like desire. I know I feel it. Every time I'm around him my body purrs to life and I feel like I can't get enough. It's always been that way, from the moment I met him.

"All alone, I'm afraid. You?"

"I'm here with someone," I stutter like an idiot. "My best friend, Emma. She's around here. Somewhere," I answer, as an excuse to look around for the person watching me.

"Ahh. In that case, care to join me for some spiced apple cider?" He points to the vendor stall in front of us selling the steaming, festive liquid that's sure to warm my chilled body.

"Yeah, I think that would be okay. If it's not weird for you."

"Nothing has felt more natural," he says in a whisper that's carried off with the wind. I'm not sure I was even supposed to hear it. Even if the feeling of eyes on me has subsided, I look around once more for anyone off in the distance before following Wes to get in line for a drink. Mind firmly back in the present, I take in the man before me. He's wearing a pair of denim jeans with black boots and a navy flannel button-up with a black puffy vest. The tattoos on his neck creep out above the top of his shirt, and it takes all of my self-control not to ask to see them, wondering if he'd let me trace my fingers along every line.

"How are you, Lilith? Enjoying yourself?"

The deep timbre of his voice pulls me from my fantasy and I shake my head lightly.

"Are you kidding? I live for this. I'm just trying to soak it all in before it's over."

"It's my favorite, too. Something about everything around us slowly dying only to come back renewed in the spring."

His response quiets me, stunned by the contemplative thought he gave it. He's exactly right. There's something so beautiful about everything being stripped bare, to survive the harsh winter, only to come back to life renewed. I stare up at him and admire his features, his chestnut hair, gorgeous brown eyes, and full beard that I want to feel against my sensitive skin. My mind spirals back into the fantasy, one I've replayed before, of his face between my legs, his tattooed hands holding me down while he brings me to orgasm with his mouth. My heart beats rapidly in my chest, thoughts of a potential ghost or stalker, or even Emma, long gone.

All that's left is Wes.

CHAPTER 5

Wes

The line inches forward as she studies me. When the silence goes on for a bit too long, I speak up. "What's that look for?" I ask, pulling her from her thoughts. Her cheeks are flushed in a gorgeous pink that isn't from the chilly night air. It looks a whole hell of a lot like arousal, and fuck if that doesn't excite me.

"Nothing, just surprised, I guess. That's a perfect way to look at the changing seasons. Way to change my outlook, Mr. Draven."

"Please don't call me, Mr. Draven, Lilith."

"Well, if I don't call you Wes and I don't call you Mr. Draven, what should I call you?"

Daddy.

"Wes will do. It isn't weird. Calling me Mr. Draven feels weird."

"Fine, I give in, Wes."

You will in time.

We reach the booth and order two spiced apple ciders plus two apple cinnamon donuts, and find a spot at a free picnic table. When she sets her bag on top of the table, a single rose tumbles out, and my lips twitch in satisfaction. She picks it up quickly, pushing it back into her bag and wincing. I look down at her hand, a red drop pooling on the pad of her thumb. She lifts her hand toward her mouth when my hand shoots out around her wrist, pulling it to me. Her eyelids lower as she watches me, tracking my movement. It takes every ounce of restraint not to bring her finger to my lips and lick it clean of her lifeblood. Instead, I take one of the napkins and press it down onto the cut.

"Secret admirer? That's a very clear sign of love from the giver," I tease, watching the spot on the napkin that turns bright red. I fold the napkin once more and lay it down again, holding pressure on her small wound. In theory, she's absolutely fine, no one ever died from a thorn prick, but I'll use any excuse to touch her, to let her feel my touch.

"You're a private investigator, right?" she asks out of nowhere.

"I am."

"What do you know about . . ." She stops talking and pulls her bottom lip into her mouth, hesitating. I give her hand a little shake, pulling her attention back to me.

"What do I know about what, Lilith? Ask." Ask me anything.

"Nothing, it's silly. The creepiness of the season has gone to my head."

"There's nothing wrong with giving in to the spookiness of the season. How is your cider?"

"Delicious, better than anything. Yours?"

"It's good. But I can think of a few things that taste better."

Your pussy.

Her face flushes, the light of the lantern illuminating the glow of the color rising on her flesh.

"There you are!" a female screeches from across the street, looking directly at Lilith.

"My best friend, Emma. I should probably go. Thank you for this, Wes," she says as her face blushes again and she gives me a devilish smile.

"I'll see you soon, Lilith."

Tonight, while you sleep in your bed.

CHAPTER 6

lily

I HUSTLE ACROSS THE STREET TO MY BEST FRIEND AS she crosses her arms and pushes out her hip, giving me a knowing smile. I loop my arm through hers, dragging her down the sidewalk, and give one last look behind us to find Wes still sitting at the picnic table, his eyes following us, with a smirk plastered on his gorgeous face. Emma starts to pull herself away from me but I tighten my hold on the menace.

"What are you doing? Let's go back! I want to have cider with Mr. Sexy."

"Don't you dare! Emma!"

I pull at her arm, refusing to let go of my grasp. The last thing I need is her going over to Wes and asking him a bunch of inappropriate questions. She gives in to me, belly laughing at my expense as I drag her away and up the street to different vendors.

"So sensitive, babe! I wasn't really going to talk to him. But seeing your reaction was well worth the threat. You're totally blushing by the way. It looked like you two were lost in your own little bubble."

It's hard not to get defensive. There's nothing going on between Wes and I—as much as I wish otherwise—it's completely one-sided, no matter how flirty his behavior can be sometimes.

"We were not. We ran into each other again and he offered to buy me a drink. I was heading to get one anyway."

"So you decided to have a little picnic together after?"

"It wasn't like that. Emma, there is nothing going on there, so no more fishing for tea that isn't there."

Her head tilts to the side, her eyes narrowing as she studies me, and I know I'm fucked.

"Oh. My. God. You're actually into him. Like more than just physical."

"What? Are you insane? That couldn't be further from the truth." But even as I say the words, they turn to ash on my tongue. She sees right through my bullshit, too.

"Look, babe, I just want you to be happy and enjoy the type of relationship you want and deserve. No more asshats like Adam."

"You're ridiculous, but I love you for it. Now, I'm craving some of Bean Haven's maple bacon donuts."

"Some as in more than one? Those things are huge."

"I said what I said, now let's go find their tent."

Emma and I stay at the harvest festival into the late evening, eating a ridiculous amount of autumn-inspired food and drinks. Around midnight, I walk down Main Street to the very end of downtown and grab my keys from my purse to unlock the door. Once inside my apartment, I kick off my boots, my feet sore from being on them the entire day, and head straight to my bathroom for a shower to warm up my body. I walk through my apartment, looking around for any sign of an intruder, or a sign that they were here while I was out, but come up short. For some reason, disappointment washes over me. A part of me hoped for another rose or sign.

Stripping my clothes off and throwing them into the laundry basket in my closet, I turn the shower on as hot as it will go, letting my bathroom fill with steam while I tie up my hair in a high bun to keep it from getting wet. I step in, adjusting the temperature, and relax into the hot water as it cascades over my body, my mind drifting from my possible stalker to Wes. There's something about him that pulls me in, and it's hard to explain. I don't realize I go through my days on edge, uptight and on my game, projecting the good girl image that my parents expect of me. Most days I feel like a circus monkey, simply showing my face and doing what I'm told. When I'm with Wes, I feel whole, my truest self. Emma was right, it's like our own little bubble. Once I step inside, I don't have to be anything but myself. He looks at me like he sees right through all of the bullshit without judgment. It's so freeing to just be able to *exist*.

I finish my shower and step out, drying myself with a fluffy towel, moisturizing, and completing my nighttime routine. I climb into my warm bed, pulling just a sheet over me since the heat in my apartment bakes my second-floor bedroom. Suddenly, my phone chimes with a text notification.

D.I.L.F: You looked beautiful tonight.

My cheeks flame and my heartbeat picks up its pace.

Me: Thank you. You looked pretty good yourself, old man.

D.I.L.F: Little girl, I'm far from old

Little girl. Why do I like that so much? I read over it three more times, each time bringing a wave of arousal over me. I wonder what it would be like to hear those words straight from his lips.

Me: You're almost 20 years older than me, I'd say that's kinda old

D.I.L.F: Experienced is a better word.

My pussy throbs.

Me: You definitely look like you know a thing or two . . .

D.I.L.F: Oh, I promise you I do. Things that would blow your mind

Holy hell. There's no misinterpreting the innuendo here. Wes Draven is flirting with me. I melt into my mattress. Before I have the nerve to respond, he texts again.

D.I.L.F: Sleep well, Lilith. I hope you have good dreams.

I fall asleep feeling needy, my head looping thoughts of Wes on repeat.

CHAPTER 7

WES

I stand in the tree line behind Lilith's apartment, waiting for all of the lights to go out and for her to be sound asleep in her bed before I break in. Security isn't an issue in Aspen Ridge, which makes slipping into places you're meant to stay out of quite easy. In fact, not including the kidnapping of Ivy Turner, we haven't had a violent or major crime in several decades. The most exciting thing that the Aspen Ridge police department has to deal with is bored teenagers throwing ragers in the woods, bonfires on Grace Beach, and underage drinking.

Being out in public with her at the harvest festival was as natural as fucking her will be. The conversation flows easily, playfully, and I wonder if she's ever had someone she can be herself with. I can't imagine what it must feel like to carry the weight of having to meet your parents' expectations constantly. I'm no parenting aficionado, but I wouldn't force Adam to be something he's not for my benefit. I may think he makes sheep-like decisions when it comes to his blind faith and stupid life choices, but I would never force him into a role that wasn't wanted.

When enough time has passed, I slip across the dark lawn, scale up the side of the apartment via the trellis, and into the unlocked window. It's the early hours of the morning when I slip into her room to watch her beautiful form sleep soundlessly in her bed. I know she feels me watching her. She always does. My pretty little temptress. She'll wake up and think it was all a dirty dream, but I know she feels my presence as much as I feel hers. I'm as real to her in her sleep as she is to me while I'm awake, watching her.

Her long, toned legs peek out from under her blanket, and my eyes roam from her sexy black-painted toes all the way up to her thighs and the curve of her hip before her body disappears back under her blanket. I can almost make out the sexy red panties she's wearing, and my cock stirs to life in my jeans. I love her subtle, private little acts of defiance—black toenails, red panties— she's not the town sweetheart that her parents pressure her into portraying, she's my dirty little girl, and once I unleash the dark side she keeps locked up tight, she'll realize how good life can be. She needs to be set free, and I'm just the man to do it.

She stirs, rolling over onto her back, and the blanket falls free from her body, exposing her to me. My mouth waters as my eyes rake over her sexy form. Her knees fall open, giving me a perfect view of her panty-clad pussy. The satin material clings to her tightly, outlining her sweet lips. Her body is stretched out in front of me like the most delicious dessert. I stand from my nightly spot in the corner chair in her room and walk closer to her, examining the silky, unmarred flesh of her body. My fingers act on their own, reaching out to touch her intimately for the first time. Ever so gently, I drag the pad of my finger up the center of her cunt, my eyes unable to look anywhere but where I'm touching her. I swipe again, adding a little more pressure. Her hips move ever so slightly, a deep sigh releasing from her lips.

Goddess.

She's not of this Earth.

So perfect.

I continue my ministrations, focusing on the little bundle of nerves at the top of her slit. Gently, I rub small circles, her hips moving every so often, her panties darkening at her slit where wetness pools. Fuck I want to taste her. I want her cum in my mouth like I need air to breathe. I need to be consumed by her. A quiet moan hits my ears and I finally look up at her face, her eyes are still closed, but her breathing is shallow, ragged. She's going to come. Give it to me, little one. I want nothing more. I chance pressing a little harder, swirling in little circles, the wetness coating all of her now, leaking through the satin fabric and coating the pad of my finger.

Her body stiffens, her abs contract, and I know I've got her. She jerks ever so slightly, her legs shaking as her body gives in to the sensation, the orgasm taking over and vibrating through her. Fuck, she's so pretty. Once her body slackens and her breathing levels out, I remove my finger, bringing it to my nose first and inhaling the sweet smell of her cunt. I fill my lungs with her before licking my finger, sucking it into my mouth. Her taste is enough to make me crazy but not enough to satiate the feral desire within me. I need it from the source.

My cock throbs painfully against the zipper of my jeans, my mouth watering with a craving so deep it's difficult to deny.

Just as I've done nights before, I unbutton my jeans and slowly slide down the zipper, pulling them down just enough to release my cock, letting it spring free as it throbs at my navel. I give a languid stroke from base to tip, holding back a groan as my palm glides over my engorged head. I can't wait for her to feel me inside her. I know it's going to drive her fucking mad. I'm long and thick and her tiny body will have to work overtime to adjust to me. I can't wait to break her in. I walk forward to the end table and pump a few squirts of her body lotion into my hand before bringing it to my face to inhale. Fuck, I love her scent. Floral and sage. So clean and innocent.

All the things that she's not.

I use the lotion to work my hand over my shaft, wanting to be covered in everything that is her. I study her sleeping face, her wavy raven hair sprawled out across her pillow, begging to be wrapped around my fist, and her dark, long eyelashes that I know are hiding the most exquisite eyes. Her skin is flawless, and all I want to do is dirty her up. I pump my cock faster, squeezing the head on every pass. The image of what it will be like to tie her down and fuck her ruthlessly appears in my head. I'm eager to kiss the burn marks around her wrists that the ropes will leave while I rut into her like the savage I am. I know she's going to love being at my mercy. My perfect little girl needs to be rumpled up, and I plan to give her everything she needs. Daddy will provide everything she needs. I stroke myself and imagine it's her cunt I'm fucking into, her walls milking the cum out of me, her body eager to be filled by me. My orgasm slams into me out of nowhere and I spill into my palm, ropes of warm, creamy cum that only belong to her. I steady my breathing, letting myself come down from the high before wiping my fingers through the mess in my hand. Leaning forward, I drag them lightly across her plump pink lips so it's not a complete waste. Don't worry, lover, you'll be completely covered in it soon enough.

Before leaving her apartment, I place a red rose on the top of her end table, a little gift for her to wake up to. Out of the corner of my eye, I see a flash of red on the top of her laundry basket. Picking up the delicate scrap of lace, I bring it to my nose and inhale her rich, sweet scent. Shoving them into my pocket, I leave my little one sleeping soundly in her bed.

CHAPTER 8

lily

MY ALARM GOES OFF WELL BEFORE I'M READY TO WAKE for the day. My sleep was haunted again by dreams of Wes Draven. They are always the same, Wes sneaking into my bedroom deep into the night, watching me, touching me until he brings me to orgasm. I stay asleep, scared that if I were to wake up he would stop and leave me unsatisfied. They're so vivid, the orgasms so real, that every morning I have to question my reality.

Reaching out to my end table, I blindly slap around for my phone to get the blaring, annoying ringing to stop. On my second slap, my palm comes down hard on spikes, and I jerk my hand back with a loud, surprised yelp. Sitting up quickly, my body freezes as I take in the sight in front of me. Sitting right next to my blaring, vibrating phone, plain as day, is a single, long-stemmed red rose.

With shaky hands, I reach forward to grab the flower, and my phone to silence it. I bring the delicate petals to my nose and inhale the sweet fragrance, a rush of excitement and terror battling for dominance inside me. I can't help but wonder if this is the start of something enchanting or something much more sinister. I know I should call the police, call my parents or Emma, but I can't shake the feeling of longing for the person who was in my room and left this for me.

After getting ready for the day, I pack up my laptop and head to Bean Haven for a latte and to get some work done. I lock up my apartment and walk down the quaint cobblestone sidewalk, kicking my boots through the dry autumn leaves and loving the noise of the rustling. A thick layer of clouds covers our small town, cocooning us in an autumn chill. It won't be much longer before the first snow comes, officially putting an end to my favorite season of the year.

Despite the familiar walk to the coffee shop, I feel a heavy presence surrounding me. That ominous thrill is like an old friend at this point, and I can't help but wonder if the secret of my stalker will be unveiled or if this is all it will ever be. The latter possibility disappoints me. I open the door to Bean Haven, the bell chiming over my head and the warmth from the shop assaulting my face. I stop in my tracks when my eyes immediately go to Wes. He's sitting at one of the few tables by himself with a laptop, a coffee, and a mouthwatering Bean Haven signature—an apple cinnamon muffin. He's wearing a black sweater —which clings to his body in all the right places—with the sleeves pushed up to his elbows, exposing the thick lines of ink that cover his corded arms and hands. Just looking at him leaves me breathless, my mind hazy, and warmth slinks through my veins until it reaches my core. The yearning I have for him is strong, but I shake my head slightly, pulling myself out of my lust-driven craving, and walk up to the counter to place my order.

Hannah works the counter like an expert, her violet hair dancing around her shoulders in loose waves. She fits the boho vibe of the coffee shop she's overhauled and updated from her grandmother perfectly.

"Hey, Lily, latte?"

"Hey, Hannah. Pumpkin spice and an apple cinnamon muffin if you have any?"

"Just sold the last one to Mr. Draven over there. Sorry. Anything else?"

Disappointment falls over me. I stick to ordering just the latte and pay, turning to find a place to sit and work when I find Wes' eyes on me. He motions for me to take the spot across from him, and heat instantly pools between my legs. Which seems to be my body's natural response to this large, tattooed, gorgeous man. Picking up my to-go mug of the sweet autumn nectar, I walk across the shop to greet him and sit down.

"Good morning, Wes."

"Good morning, Lilith. How was your night?"

His question stuns me before I realize that's a perfectly normal thing to ask someone first thing in the morning. It's impossible for him to know of my erotic dreams that took center stage the entire night. With him as the star.

"It was incredible," I tell him truthfully. He smirks at me with a devilish grin before pushing his small plate in my direction. My eyes dip down to the apple cinnamon muffin sitting untouched, then slide to his hand. His thick fingers are covered in tattoos that spread across the top and over his wrist in an intricate design. I lift my eyes to find his already on me, his focus so strong that it nearly forces the air from my lungs.

"Hungry?" he finally asks, not breaking eye contact.

"It's yours, I'm okay," I answer, my voice shaky from being under his powerful stare.

"I overheard you order one though, please. I want you to have it."

"That's sweet, Wes, but it's yours. You enjoy it."

"I will enjoy it more if I get to watch you eat it, knowing I'm the reason behind your pleasure."

Any coherent thought I could have conjured eludes me as I take in this perfect man in front of me and what he just said.

I will enjoy it more if I get to watch you eat it, knowing I'm the reason behind your pleasure.

All I can do is smile and nod my head in agreement. His face brightens, his smile turning up, and his eyes squinting slightly, crinkling the skin at the corners. He pulls his hand back, running it through his thick beard, and my eyes track the motion, wondering what it would feel like if it was my hand instead of his own.

"Are you excited about tomorrow?" he asks, breaking me from my haze. I take a sip of my latte before picking off a piece of the crumbling streusel topping.

"I am. It's my favorite day of the year. Anything goes on Halloween, and I tend to lean into it. What about you?"

"I've never been more excited about anything."

"You must have some special plans then," I joke, a bit of jealousy coursing through me like a disease. The thought of Wes with someone else leaves a sick feeling in the pit of my stomach, like I swallowed battery acid.

"I do." The look he gives me as he says those two words ignites the flutter of butterflies throughout my body. It was delivered in a way that sounded not like a statement or fact, but a promise.

We work across from each other for the next several hours in comfortable silence. I glance up from my computer every few minutes, his presence both a calming balm to my nervous system and the reason my heart hasn't slowed down in excitement.

I run last-minute errands the rest of the day, and by the evening I'm so eager for tomorrow and all of its possibilities, that I eat a quick meal and take a long, hot bath to help me relax. My mind never strays from Wes, my stalker, and the foreboding feeling that's been haunting me for weeks.

Feeling like tempting fate tonight, I walk through my apartment in nothing but a silk robe that hangs to the top of my thighs, barely covering my ass. I open the back door to my apartment, stepping out into the cool autumn night, the cold hardwood of the small deck chilling me through my bare feet. I look around the backyard, finding it peacefully empty. With shaky fingers, I untie my robe, letting the fabric fall open, exposing my naked body underneath. I trail my fingers down my neck, over the divots of my collarbone, and between my breasts before turning and walking inside. Instead of locking my door like I always do, I leave it unlocked, walking straight to my bedroom like a fucking crazy person.

CHAPTER 9

WES

THE DAY I'VE PLANNED ENDLESSLY FOR IS ALMOST HERE. Tomorrow, at the abandoned asylum, I will finally bring Lilith into the darkness with me. I'll make her mine whether she likes it or not. I know she may fight it at first, knowing how wrong it is, but I know she wants me. I see it in the way her eyes rake up my body when she thinks I'm not looking, the way her eyes hold mine for a beat longer than she should. The way she comes for me in her sleep. But first, I need to see her. Need to taste her once more while she sleeps.

I sneak into her apartment unscathed as I've done every other night since finding out she was no longer having her time wasted with my son. This time though, I walk through the back door that she left unlocked for me. Well, not *me*, but her stalker. I watched her from the woods, standing behind the tree line, concealed by the darkness of the trees as she tempted me. The succubus called me to her. I would have dropped to my knees and crawled across her godforsaken lawn if she wanted me to. The only thing holding me back was my desire to see my plans through. To take her as my own on her favorite night of the year.

All of the lights are off, the apartment pitch black, but I know my way around in the dark by now. I navigate through her living room, up the stairs, and down the small hallway into the open door of her bedroom. Her curtains are open, the moon shining a silver light and illuminating her body, which lies peacefully on top of her bed. She looks like a sleeping goddess lying on her altar. Her body is covered by just a thin sheet, draped over the curves of her perfect skin, leaving nothing to the imagination.

I take a seat in a chair that sits in the corner of her room, enveloped by the shadows, and watch. It amazes me how deep of a sleeper she is, and I wonder if I were to fuck her right now if she'd even become conscious.

She rolls over, moving from her side to her stomach, her hands pushing under her pillow, and her knee moving out to the side. The blankets roll with her, exposing her entire naked body to me. Her perky ass is on display and spread open. My cock hardens to steel, throbbing painfully. Too enraptured by the sight in front of me, I pay him no mind. I stand, quietly moving closer to the bed to look at my goddess.

"Wes," she moans softly, barely audible. "Please. Touch me."

Her eyes are closed, her breathing shallow and soft, when I realize she's dreaming of me. Her hips grind lightly into the mattress. It's not just any dream though, my dirty little girl is having a sex dream about me. Unable to deny her request, I kneel on the bed, inching forward slowly before slipping my hand under her pussy, wedging it between her core and the bed. My fingers slide through her slick folds like warm butter. She's bare of any hair, her skin smooth and soft.

Her hips continue to move and rotate against my hand in a tortuously slow rhythm, but my fingers sink right between her wet folds, pressing against her little clit, moisture dripping down from her core coating them, allowing her to move with gentle ease. With her knee pressed out high to the side, she's completely exposed to me. My mouth waters as I stare at her pink slit and tight little asshole. My heart beats wildly in my chest as I watch her chase her pleasure, her subconscious leading her dreams to exactly what she wants, what she needs.

Having observed her long enough now, I know that she sleeps like the dead, and I decide I can't hold back completely any longer. Giving in to my primal desires, I lean forward and drag the tip of my tongue through her pussy and up to her ass. Her flavor explodes on my tongue. Light and sweet, like the most desired ambrosia of the gods. Her hips continue their slow rock on my hand and I decide to take more. *I need more.*

I lean in, rimming her tight puckered hole with my tongue, letting the spit fall from my mouth and gather at the spot. Her hips move with more force, my fingers brushing that swollen nub, her climax climbing higher and higher. I eat her asshole like the savage I am, devouring her in any possible way that I can. I need any piece of her. I need all of her. I press my tongue in, swirling it around the rim as she starts to orgasm. Her body jerks, her legs shaking as the waves of pleasure pulse through her tight little silhouette, my name whispered on her tongue.

My hand is flooded with warm cum and I slowly pull it out from under her as her body relaxes. Standing, I use my free hand to pull myself free from my pants, grabbing my hard cock with the hand coated in her moisture, smearing it all over me, loving this connection to her. I grip my dick tightly, stroking it wildly while staring at her plump pussy and little asshole, still glistening from my saliva. The urge to climb on top of her, grab her hips, and thrust my cock deep inside her tight cunt is strong. The only thing holding me back is that she's asleep. I want her eyes on me the first time I take her. I want her to watch as I claim her body for my own. Watch how I fill her wholly and completely. My cock strains in my palm and I tighten my hold, twisting my hand over the head on every upstroke. My balls draw up as my cock thickens, and right before I come, I lean into her, as close as I can get without touching her, and let go. White, pearly streams of cum pulse out of me and onto her waiting pussy and asshole, sticking to her flushed skin like the most beautiful accessory.

She looks fucking beautiful like this, more gorgeous and addictive than I could have ever imagined. I tuck myself back into my jeans, admiring my decoration between her legs. My cum has seeped in, mixing with her own. I give myself one last treat, leaning my mouth in and licking light strokes, cleaning her up of the mess. The combined taste of both our releases on my tongue is euphoric. This will be my favorite dessert.

I slip back into the shadows of her room, taking my seat in the chair, and get comfortable, ready to spend the next few hours watching my little one sleep. I think about my plan for Halloween and how she'll react when she finds out the truth. She might fight it. She might be angry. But in time she'll realize that we're meant to be together. She was made for me. Societal norms be damned. Before leaving, I place the red rose on the pillow next to her head.

I've kept my distance long enough, but that all ends tonight.

Tomorrow, I bring my Lilith into the darkness with me.

Tomorrow, I make her mine.

See you soon, little one.

lily

I STARE AT MYSELF IN MY FULL-LENGTH MIRROR, rethinking the costume I chose. The white corset top hugs my chest and gives me more cleavage than I thought possible with my small breasts. It cinches tightly around my waist before flaring out slightly at my hips in a tiny lace skirt that hits mid-thigh. It leaves little to the imagination, but that was the whole point. The matching wings I'll put on when I get to the party are massive and filled with gorgeous white feathers, bringing the entire costume together. It doesn't exactly scream "first date" but it's a costume party, and I'm rocking it. I'm going as an angel, and the irony of it isn't lost on me.

I may project that persona to the outside world, thanks to my parents, but there's a part of me I keep hidden that yearns for the dark and depraved. I'm sure my date tonight will be another dud, just like the last dozen. They're always the same—pretty, rich, kind, and considerate. They ask all the right questions, do all the right things, and look at me like I'm a precious, delicate little flower. Which is great, if you're into that. It's exactly what my parents want for me. What they expect. While the guys may be stable and sweet, when I imagine the future with each of them, I picture coffee at opposite ends of the table every morning while we watch the news, Tuesday missionary sex at 9 p.m., and a mundane life rotating around each other's work and social obligations.

If my husband doesn't want to bend me over the kitchen counter and fuck me like he can't start his day without filling me first, then I don't want it. I don't want to be fucked like I'm breakable. When I finally got the courage and told Adam I wanted him to get rough with me during a blowjob and chase his own pleasure, he was appalled. He told me that he could never violate me like that. Violate me. Like I wasn't begging him for it and the thought of it didn't drench my panties. Even if I was thinking about his dad the entire time. I know, hell. I'm bound for it.

I pull out my phone and snap a photo to send to Emma, wanting her opinion. Not that I have another option at this point.

> Emma: You look hot AF

> Me: Yeah?

> Emma: Yeah, I'd do you

> Me: If you didn't like dick so much

> Emma: Yeah I can't give that up. The more the merrier.

Deciding that I agree with Emma, I throw on my heels, grab my jacket, wings, and purse, and head to the door. The cold air hits my lungs as I walk into the crisp Halloween night, garnering the attention of two men on the short walk to my car, which fuels my confidence. With my black Honda Civic in sight, my breath catches in my lungs. On the windshield, is another single red rose, this one wilted around the delicate petals. Having finally learned my lesson from the previous times, I carefully pick up the stem without being cut and bring it to my nose to smell. I look around the long, busy street of downtown, my head swiveling, searching for whoever is lurking in the dark.

Once safely in my car, my phone chimes again with a text. Pulling it out, my body breaks out in goosebumps, my pussy throbbing. The response is primal and uncontrolled and hits me like a tidal wave.

D.I.L.F: Be safe tonight.

Me: What fun is that, Mr. Draven?

Wanting nothing more than to toy with this man, no matter how wrong it is, I send the flirty text, turn my phone on vibrate, and start the drive into the Pacific Northwest woods. The night is dark, the trees tall and domineering, casting wild shadows over the narrow road, and creating the sensation of driving through a tunnel. The air is heavy with an eerie stillness, as if the world around me is holding its breath, waiting for something ominous and sinister to unfold. The long, winding road stretches in front of me, curving around bends, darkness swallowing everything around me, the full moon ahead illuminating my destination like a beacon in the sinister Halloween night. It's hauntingly beautiful. I love it.

I park my little car among the lines of others here for a night of carefree fun with the tortured souls trapped within these forsaken walls. The abandoned insane asylum sits at the very end of a long dirt road that's only visible because of the cars that blazed the trail ahead of me. The landscape is overgrown and dying, the air thick with the scent of decay and despair.

I step through the crumbling entrance, a feeling of unease settling over me. A chill sweeps through, sending shivers down my spine and goosebumps up my arms. I look around again, knowing that eyes in the distance are tracking my every move. I play coy, facing back toward the darkness and pulling my bottom lip between my teeth. I lift my pointer finger and move it in a "come here" motion. When they don't give anything away, I quicken my pace and enter the building. The music from the DJ consumes every sound, the bass taking over my heartbeat, forcing it to the rhythm of the beat. I continue to walk through the asylum, and see the center has been turned into a massive dance floor. People from every town in our area fill the space, dancing and letting loose, letting themselves escape on the best evening of the year. But I couldn't shake the feeling that tonight was about to change everything for me.

I find the makeshift bar and walk over, realizing now that I left my wings in the car, along with my purse. I take one step before someone appears in front of me. I register his face from his photo and am thankful he wasn't using a fake. He's slightly taller than me, athletic build, in a basic Clark Kent costume. He's completely clean-shaven and looks exactly like someone my parents would set me up with.

"Lily?"

He's attractive enough, tall and fit, his near-black hair combed over and gelled in the Superman style. His suit is clearly tailored, and not of the costume variety. I imagine that his Clark Kent look is not too far off from his day-to-day Marcus look.

"Yes. Marcus?"

"Correct. It's good to finally meet you. My parents have been raving about you."

I internally cringe. I'm so over my parents trying to set me up with men from their elite inner circle. They're all the same. I straighten my spine and decide it's better to just go with it. It's my favorite night of the year and I'm not going to let anything get me down. He can get on board with that or find someone else to spend his time with tonight.

"How about a drink? I could use one."

"First date nerves?" he asks, and I do everything I can not to roll my eyes.

"I guess you could say that. Beer is fine."

He walks away for a moment and returns with two clear plastic cups full of beer from the keg. I take one from his hand and down half of it.

"Easy, angel. I want to get to know you. Want to go somewhere to sit and talk?" he asks as he looks around in disgust. This is clearly not his vibe. Knowing he doesn't mean to hook up and that he genuinely wants to leave the area to talk, I make a different suggestion, because tonight is mine.

"How about we dance?" Not waiting for an answer, I leave him where he stands and saunter to the makeshift dance floor. "Closer" by Nine Inch Nails blares from the speakers around me and I let myself go to it. My hips sway side to side, my hands moving through my hair and back down, letting my fingers trail over the skin on my neck—the sensual dance of someone who doesn't care if anyone is watching but secretly hopes all eyes are on her.

It's not long before someone slinks up behind me, and based on their size, it's not Marcus. But there isn't a single part of me that cares at this moment. This is my night. The one night of the year when I completely let go and let myself be who I wish I could be every other day, too.

The song changes and I let myself go to the rhythm of "For Your Entertainment" by Adam Lambert. The lyrics roll over me, and my mind drifts to my stalker, wondering if he's here, if he's watching.

Hoping that he is.

CHAPTER 11

WES

I LEAN AGAINST THE DECREPIT WALL FACING THE DANCE floor to finish my beer and watch as Lilith and some asshole dance. She's wearing a pure, white angel costume that I internally laugh at. She's anything but, and I can't wait to show her.

Making my plan for tonight was easy after reading her messages. But the man she's dancing with isn't Marcus dearest. This man is ballsier than the pussy who left her. He pulls her hips flush against him, one knee pressing between her legs as they grind on each other and sway to the music. She's smiling up at him and the jealousy courses through me. I'm the only one who gets her smiles. I'm debating how long to wait before I go to her when Lilith's eyes meet mine from across the room. Her guileless, hazel eyes flash with excitement and temptation. Her hands work through his hair and then she pulls his face into her neck, a challenge to me, daring me to intervene, not a hint of reservation on her pretty face. He responds by dragging his hands up her waist to the sides of her breasts and back down to her hips. She knows she's playing with fire right now. My little one wants to tempt me, see what I'll do. Little does she know she's about to have all of me, and she'll never have anyone else after me.

I watch as she sways her body into the fucker who's touching what's mine. She's completely lost to the beat of the music now, her eyes closing as she moves her head side to side with the rhythm. I adjust my hard cock that's pressing painfully against my jeans. She's so fucking sexy. So mine. I'm dying to claim her.

The beast in me calls to her and I can't let another man touch what's mine a second longer. Before I know it, my feet are leading me in her direction, unable to fight the pull. I slip in easily behind her, and she immediately drops her head back on my chest, my hands resting on her tight waist. The piece of shit in front of her doesn't take the hint and stays glued to her front. He leans forward, mouth open as if to kiss along her neck when I reach my hand out and snag the front of his shirt, jerking him forward into us. Lilith rears back further into me as she gasps, her hands coming up between them.

"Touch her again and I swear it'll be the last fucking thing you do." His eyes bug out of his head but he releases his hold on my woman and runs off like the pathetic piece of shit he is. I grip my fingers around her hip and pull her ass further into me so that my hard cock can rub against her lower back. Her breathing settles and she starts to move her hips in a sexy, sensual sway to the beat pulsing around us.

"Naughty girl," I whisper in her ear. "You like playing with fire, Lilith?"

"What if I do?" she challenges. This woman is so perfect for me, and she doesn't even realize it yet.

"Little girl, you're about to find out."

She turns in my arms and meets my eyes. Lust-filled, hazy from the bit of alcohol she's consumed, and so goddamn fucking beautiful. Holding her in my arms feels like the universe just came together in a cosmic event. Like everything is finally how it should be. My little she-demon wrapped up tightly with me.

"Show me, Mr. Draven."

I pull her hips flush against me before gripping a handful of her long hair and forcing her head back. She hisses through her teeth but doesn't break eye contact with me. I lean forward slowly, holding her still, letting my beard rub against the delicate skin of her neck before licking up the length. The saltiness of her sweat coats my tongue before I suck her earlobe between my teeth. She moans, soft and sultry. Her hand makes a fist in my shirt and grips me like she doesn't want to let me go. She's in for a surprise. I whisper into her ear, causing her to shiver and break out in goosebumps.

"I'm going to make you wish you never challenged me. Now, we're going to play a little game. When I say so, you're going to hide. Any floor but this one, I want you away from all of these people." Her little intake of air sends a jolt right to my already hard cock. "When I find you, and I *will* find you, I'm going to claim my prize. Do you know what that is?"

She shakes her head, her eyes heavy and wild.

"I'm going to force your dark side out to play, little one. I'm going to show you how good it can feel when you give in to the darkness inside you. I'm going to fuck you so good I'll be all you think about. All you want. All you *need*."

Not that I have plans to ever be away from her again after tonight. But she doesn't need to know that right now.

"Tell me you understand the rules, Lilith." I look down at her face that's flushed with arousal, excitement, and trepidation. Her pulse pounds erratically under my finger at her neck.

"Ye-yes."

I slam my lips down on hers, tightening my hold on her hair and angling her head exactly where I want her. I devour her mouth, forcing her lips to part so that I can taste her for the first time. She mewls into my mouth the moment my tongue meets hers, her body rubbing against mine like a cat. The kiss is aggressive. Bruising. Finally unleashed after weeks of pent-up tension and anticipation. I lick into her mouth, tasting her and loving the feel of her in my arms. I suck her tongue into my mouth before claiming her lips again. She tastes sweet like honey, addictive and consuming. I pull her plump bottom lip between my teeth, dragging them across her smooth flesh as I pull away with a little pop.

She looks up at me, lust-drunk as a drop of blood pools on the corner of her mouth. I wipe my thumb across it, collecting the blood on the pad of my finger and bringing it in front of my face to examine it. I meet her eyes as I suck my finger into my mouth and moan. Her eyes glaze over, heated and eager. Good. I reach between us to palm her pussy, not giving a shit that we're on a dance floor surrounded by people. "I can't wait to show this pussy how a real man should treat it. I'm going to have it leaking my cum for days."

I peck her lips once more before meeting her eyes straight on. "Run."

lily

I HESITATE FOR A SPLIT SECOND BEFORE TURNING OUT of Wes' hold and walking quickly through the crowd of people to the old crumbling stairs that lead to the second floor. *Run.* His voice echoes in my mind, a steady, ominous command. My mind struggles to catch up with reality. I can't believe this is happening. I thought the tension between Wes and I was all in my head, that it was one-sided, even though my body felt like he was interested. Maybe tonight is the same for him, just one night a year that he lets himself be free to enjoy whatever he wants, no matter how wrong or off-limits that may be.

There's a part of me that knows I should be running for help, running to my car at least, but the other part of me—a larger part of me that I can't ignore—wants this. I want him to chase me, to see what he'll do once he finds me. I want to be hunted. I *need* him to expose the dark side of me.

Goosebumps scatter across my skin as the feeling of being watched returns. I know he can see me as I carefully climb the steps, watching for holes in the slabs of rotting wood. Once I'm at the top, I turn right around a large, broken banister, and the moment I know I'm out of sight, I run. My heels echo off the ground with each step, and I race around a corner, where the space opens into an old recreation room. Tables are flipped, chairs on their sides, paper scattered everywhere, but there isn't a place to hide.

With my heart hammering in my chest, I race through the open room to another hallway filled with doors, turning into the first open one. I quickly realize I'm standing in one of the patient rooms. The walls are covered in graffiti, with dirt and grime coating every inch of the room. A dirty, stained mattress lays on the floor, the metal spring frame against one of the walls. I scurry behind the door, making myself as small as possible as I sink to the floor and pull my knees up to my chest, doing everything I can to steady my heartbeat.

Wes is an animal hunting, and I'm his prey, my fear a palpable signal leading him right to me. There's nothing else I can do but wait.

CHAPTER 13

WES

"Ready or not, here I come."

I walk through the throngs of people, taking my time. The hunt is just as good as the prize. With my hands in my pockets, I stroll up the stairs and follow the turn I watched Lilith make. Her dark floral and sage scent lightly hits my nose like the sweetest nectar. Addictive. The steady bass of the music thumps throughout the building, the perfect noise to muffle her screams from everyone partying downstairs. I reach a rec room and look around for any sign of my prey. It's quiet, not even a rustling of paper.

"Lilith . . . you can run but you can't hide," I taunt as I walk through the crumbling room and into a long hallway. Each step of my boots echoes off the quiet hallway and I hope she hears it, I hope she feels me closing in on her. I can picture her, trembling, fear dripping off her in waves, mixed with the pheromones of her arousal. My mouth salivates at the thought.

"Little girl, I know you're here somewhere. I can smell you. Practically taste you on my tongue. Come out, come out wherever you are."

Opening the first door to my right, my eyes roam the empty room, seeing nothing but a metal tray on the ground. I pull the door closed and turn to my left. A door half-hangs off the hinges, left partially open. My heart rate picks up in anticipation of catching her. She's in there. I take a step across the hallway, coming to a stop in front of the door. I close my eyes and listen, inhaling deeply as that dark incense fills my lungs.

"You know you're trapped, Lilith. I've found you," I say as I push open the door just enough to step inside. Her scream echoes loudly off the cement walls of the small room. "And now I get my prize."

I take a step into the room and don't see her, but just as I spin to turn around to face the door, she's standing and pulling the door open with force. I grab her around the waist, hauling her off her feet and into my chest.

"Oh no you don't. I've come to collect. You wanted to play and you can't get out now."

She screams and wiggles in my arms, trembling with the war of emotions going on inside her. I kick the door closed and it creaks and whines on its last hinge. Placing her back down, I spin her in my arms and kick out her feet, laying her down on a dirty mattress under me. I push her legs open and drop my hips into her, grinding my hard cock into her soft center. Gathering her wrists in my hand, I hold them above her head, spreading her out below me, at my mercy. She whimpers and my cock jerks in response.

"I want my prize, Lilith. Are you going to tell me no?"

CHAPTER 14

lily

"W e s h o u l d n ' t d o t h i s." I h e s i t a t e. I k n o w f u l l well this is a line I can't come back from if I cross it, no matter how badly I want to. Wes is Adam's dad for fuck's sake and almost twenty years older than me. It doesn't matter how long I've lusted over this man.

"Get out of your head. My son's a fucking moron, Lilith. Let me take care of this needy cunt. It's been neglected for too long. Don't think. Just feel. Let me free you . . ."

My breath gets caught in my chest as I nod, unsure if he would have stopped even if I hadn't said a single thing. Releasing my wrists, he moves down between my legs, shoving up the skirt of my costume and ripping my thin, string panties from my body. My body trembles in anticipation.

Wasting no time, he leans forward and runs his nose through my folds, inhaling deeply as he goes. His beard feathers over my sensitive skin, eliciting a spark deep in my core. My pussy throbs, aching. I reach down, running my fingers through his soft hair.

"Fuck. You smell so fucking good."

He does the movement again and again, just breathing me in. It's so filthy and erotic, and my hips move forward, chasing his mouth with the motion as he continues to inhale my scent.

The rough pads of his fingers finally touch me where I need him as he spreads my lips with his thumbs and looks at me, his face hovering over my center, eyes roaming over my dripping wet core. My knees shake, my entire body trembling. I can't take my eyes off him. I've spent so much time imagining this and it's a million times better than my dreams.

"So bare. So soft and smooth."

The rough pads of his thumbs rub up and down on my lips, continuing to spread me open to him. He blows lightly over my damp flesh, the cool air sending a shiver through my entire body. I feel my arousal dripping from me and I know he can see it as it leaks from my core down to my ass. The moan from his lips is feral, and the anticipation is killing me. I wiggle in his hold, wanting his mouth on me like I won't survive if he doesn't kiss me there.

"So needy, little girl. You want my mouth on your pussy?"

"Yes," I whine.

"Tell daddy what you need." His voice is slightly deeper than normal and there's no missing the demanding tone.

My eyes roll to the back of my head at his words. This man is everything I thought I needed and it's a million times better than I had imagined. This is my night. This is what I wanted. He sees me . . . the real me. And seems to be so attuned to exactly how I want it.

I'm going to show you how good it can feel when you give in to the darkness inside you.

I give in.

"I need you to lick me, daddy. Please," I purr.

He moans again, a deep rumble that comes from somewhere dark and hidden, before giving me what I want and dragging the flat of his tongue from my center up to my clit. Heaven. I've fucking died and gone straight to heaven. Or hell, in this case. The devil is in front of me dragging me down with him. As I lay spread open on a trashy old mattress in a room of an abandoned asylum with my ex-boyfriend's dad feasting on my core, never in my wildest dreams did I think I'd be here. If this is what hell is like, I'll gladly burn for eternity with Wes by my side.

"Fuck, you taste so good, Lilith. Pull down your top so I can see those perky tits."

I don't hesitate to listen. I pull down my corset top as best I can to free my boobs.

"Now play with them. Pinch your nipples while I eat your sweet little cunt."

I caress them with my palms before giving all my attention to my nipples. I tweak and twist until they're painfully hard. He doesn't take his eyes off me while I do, and he's yet to return his mouth to where I want it. I pinch hard on one and moan, feeling the wetness pool between my legs. He drags a finger lightly through my center, gathering up the moisture.

"That's my good girl. Your pussy is weeping for me. Fuck, I love how responsive you are. Taste how good it is."

He brings the finger covered in my essence up to my mouth and I greedily suck on it, circling my tongue around. In one quick motion, Wes grabs me by the hips and flips onto his back, lifting me on top of him and positioning my legs on either side of his head.

"What are you doing?" I ask in a panic as I try to balance and hover over him.

"You're so fucking wet. I want you to drown me in it. Now sit on my face and ride me."

Fuck. I've never had anyone want me like this. Pure, unadulterated, unhinged, primal desire. This is all I've ever wanted.

"Yes, daddy," I cry out.

A moan rumbles up from his chest.

"Fucking hell, I love it when you call me that, Lilith. Now be daddy's good girl and sit."

Wes tightens his grip on my hips before pulling my center down on his face. There's nothing for me to grab to take some of the weight off, so sit is exactly what I'm forced to do. His tongue pierces me, fucking in and out of my pussy as my hips rock back and forth on his face. His thick facial hair rubs the sensitive skin on the inside of my thighs raw, rubbing against my ass, a slight sting adding to the pleasure he's giving me. My moans echo off the walls of the room, drowned out by the music of the party below us.

"Yes! Yes! Oh, that feels so good," I scream out.

His mouth devours me. Licking through my folds like he wants to touch every part of me that he can reach. He dips back into my center before licking up to my clit and swirling his tongue around it. My hips move of their own accord, continuing to rock back and forth on his mouth as my orgasm builds and builds. His large hands hold me down on him, wrapped around my thighs to keep me exactly where he wants me.

"Oh, god, please don't stop." I'm so fucking close.

"Never. I'm never leaving. Now show me what a good pussy does when it's being taken care of. Come for daddy, let me have it," he says before sucking my swollen nub into his mouth. Hard.

I combust. Pleasure like I've never experienced before courses through my body. My toes curl, and I'm forced to fall forward and brace myself with my hands on the dirty ground over his head. He continues to hold my hip with one hand, forcing me down on his face further. The pressure of his fingers at my entrance increases the building pleasure inside of me as they curl deep within me. I spiral further into the abyss.

I feel myself gush as my orgasm peaks, pummeling through me. Tears prick my eyes, and I scream out his name. Liquid rushes from my core, squirting out in quick gushes all over his face, soaking his beard, drowning him, just like he wanted.

"WES! Fuck! Yes!!!!"

I slow my hips but Wes doesn't leave my overly sensitive pussy. He continues to lap at me languidly, like he doesn't want to waste a drop of my release.

"You did so good. Fuck, I love your tight little body."

He takes one last long lick up my center, from ass to clit, before picking me up by my waist and moving me next to him. I collapse down onto my back, my legs falling open. I look over at him, his face glistening with my cum as he smiles down at me, almost wickedly.

"Taste yourself on me," is the only warning I get before his mouth consumes me. His tongue clashes with mine, the taste of me mixing with everything that is him. I loop my arms around his neck, pulling him closer to me, my leg swinging over his hip.

I feel rabid.

Out of control.

Lost to this lust-fueled craze that he's ignited inside me. I can't get enough. He pulls back from the kiss, biting my bottom lip and dragging his teeth over the tender flesh until I taste blood. My eyes look to his lips, swollen and glossy.

"Mmm. Daddy's girl tastes so good. You ready for more, Lilith?" he asks as he adjusts my corset, pulling it back over my breasts, his rough finger trailing across my skin in a light caress that I want more of.

"Yes," I say, my voice trembling. His eyes meet mine as he looks at me like a lion would look at his prey.

"Then run," he says, his voice deep and foreboding.

There's zero hesitation this time. I clamber to my feet as quickly as I can, kicking off my heels and bolting away from him. Adrenaline pumps through my bloodstream, propelling me forward. The old hardwood floors creak under the weight of each of my steps. I race down the long hallway, the wallpaper peeling off the walls, exposing the stained, crumbling concrete behind them. I spin around a corner, rustling up old papers and documents in my wake.

A broken window has left shattered glass on the ground and I dance over it, careful not to cut my bare feet. The cold autumn breeze blows through the open window, stealing the breath from my overworked lungs. I don't stop until I come to a closed door on my right. I turn the handle to open it, but it only opens a foot, something in front of it holding it partially closed. I press against it but it won't budge. Squeezing in through the small space, I wedge myself into what appears to be an old medical room.

A hospital chair with stirrups like you'd find in a gynecologist's office sits on the far side of the room with thick restraints on each corner. My body shivers at what atrocities could have been committed in this room. A metal table is on its side, and various medical tools are tossed about on the stained floor. The wallpaper is peeling off in large ribbons, and the concrete walls are crumbling in some areas. I'm frozen for a split second as I take in the horror of the room. Finding the closet, I open it and step in, pulling it closed in front of me and peering through the slits.

"Ready or not, here I come," his voice echoes from the hallway. He's tracking me, and he's damn quick. I scoot further into the decaying structure around me, the smell of old linen and dust assaulting my nose, pulling my knees to my chest and doing my best not to make a sound.

"There's no hiding from me, Lilith. There's nowhere you can go that I won't find you. You're mine. Daddy's dirty little girl."

His boots become louder, the floor creaking and moaning as he walks casually through the dark, damp asylum. The wind howls through the shattered windows, creating a haunting symphony that fits the torment that occurred within these walls.

"I know what you need, baby. Only daddy can give it to you. I've been watching you. I know you've felt it, haven't you?"

I cover my mouth with my trembling hands, doing everything I can to steady my rapid breathing. I gasp and squeeze my hand tighter around my mouth. My fear and anticipation build, my teeth clattering together loudly. My heart beats loudly in my ears, my chest rising and falling in short, rapid breaths.

My stalker.

It was Wes the entire time. Wes was following me. Wes was leaving me roses. Wes was outside my window in the tree line that night, watching me fuck myself with my fingers. Wes was in my apartment. Wetness pools between my legs. It's been him all along. How long has he wanted me? Been stalking me? How did I miss it? Of course it's him.

"You've felt me in your dreams, too. Haven't you?"

My heart stops beating as the ringing sounds loudly between my ears.

"None of it was a dream, little one. I was there. In your room. Watching you. Smelling you. Touching you. You come so prettily when you're sleeping, lover."

A scream bursts from my lungs as the door to the office is kicked open with a loud bang, wood splintering and breaking, the hinges creaking as it crashes against the wall in front of the closet door where I'm hiding. I squeeze my mouth shut with my hands as Wes rips open the closet door, staring at me like I'm the missing key to everything he needs. His dark eyes are wild, the irises blown so big that it makes them look black.

"There's my girl." He reaches forward, wrapping a firm hand around one of my ankles and pulling, dragging me across the cold ground. I fall backward from the force, my elbows hitting first to keep my head from bouncing off the hardwood below me. I cry out but he doesn't stop until I'm splayed out on the dirty floor in front of him. Half naked. Dirty. Cold. My body trembling from the combination of fear and lust.

"It was you all along," I stutter.

"Of course it was. You think I'd let anyone else get that close to you?"

"You're fucking insane," I hiss.

He straddles my body, arm shooting out straight, his big hand splayed around my throat, squeezing just enough to garner my attention. He leans down until we're face to face, his breath warm on my skin.

"Don't pretend that you don't fucking love it. Or do. It doesn't change anything either way."

His free arm reaches behind him, fingers swiping through the center of my legs. I flinch under him and he tightens his hold around my neck, his thumb swiping lightly back and forth across my pulse point. He expertly touches my pussy, like he already knows exactly how to get me to the point of no return. His fingers glide through my slick folds, pressing down hard on my clit, rubbing circles around it, making me cry out for him. Playing me like he's done before.

"Take a deep breath, little one. It's going to feel so damn good."

I do as he says, filling my lungs with air just as his hand squeezes, cutting off my airflow. My hands fly out, grabbing around his forearm, trying to pull him off me as my head starts to spin from lack of oxygen. The fingers between my legs pinch my clit, and tears flow out of the corners of my eyes. The pressure in my chest tightens, my heartbeat a loud thump in my ears, and just as the orgasm crests and I fall off that glorious peak, he lets go of the pressure around my neck. The orgasm is bliss. I gasp for air as I scream his name, my toes curling, my body shaking as the most incredible pleasure replaces all reasonable thought. It's only this. This feeling that he gives me. This pleasure.

"That's it. Scream my name. Let everyone know who's making you feel this good."

And I do. Over and over until my body collapses. My legs fall open, limp and satiated. I vaguely hear the zipper of his pants and the rustling of clothes, my eyes too heavy to check. And then it's his warm tongue on my overly sensitive center. I quiver under him, trying to pull away, needing a moment of rest before he continues his damnation of my body.

"Please, Wes."

I peel my eyes open to find him completely naked, kneeling between my legs while he licks my pussy, his arm moving languidly between his legs, stroking himself to pleasuring me. I've never seen anything so erotic. The moon shines through the window, lighting the room just enough to put his tattooed body on display for me. He's covered. Almost every inch of his torso, arms, and neck are decorated in ink.

He licks into my center, his tongue pulsing in and out,

sending waves of pleasure through me. I reach down, tugging his chestnut hair, pulling him closer to me. The moan that rumbles through him sends shockwaves over every inch of my body.

I'm consumed.

I was right. There's no coming back from this.

CHAPTER 15

WES

I bite down on Lilith's clit as I press two fingers into her. Her back arches off the floor as she continues to writhe underneath me, pushing her pussy into my face. Goddamn, this woman.

She is so fucking hot. So responsive, so wet that she's dripping down my chin, my beard drenched with her juices. Just how I want it. I love every moment of being between her legs. I never want to come up for air. Suffocation by Lilith's sweet pussy seems like one hell of a way to go out. And as much as I want to make this last as long as possible, I'm eager to finally be inside her, my dick so hard and angry that it's painful as I stroke it in my fist.

"One more, my little demon. Give daddy one more."

Her legs tremble on either side of me, her abs contracting as her moans fill the space. Another swipe of my tongue and bite between my teeth and her walls clench tightly around my fingers, her clit swelling and throbbing hard against my tongue. She gushes, her sweet taste flooding my mouth.

"That's it. I want you messy, baby girl. I want you dripping so you're ready to take my fat cock."

"Fuck. Daddy! Wes! Fuck! Yes!" she screams.

"That's my good girl. Come for me. Let Daddy have all of it."

Her body responds so well, coming so prettily, giving me the orgasm I so desperately wanted from her. Her skin is flushed from the pleasure, makeup running from her eyes, dirt dusting her fair skin. She's never looked so raw, and I fucking love her dirtied up.

The moment her legs stop shaking I sit up on my knees, stroking my cock and sliding it back and forth through her folds, spreading my leaking precum over her sensitive, swollen cunt. She squirms, trying to force me inside her. I don't make her wait long. Grabbing her hips between my hands, I lift her ass off the floor, lining her up with my cock before driving in until I reach the hilt in one powerful thrust.

My head drops back as I feel her sheathed around me for the first time. She gasps, trying to pull away from me as her body fights to adjust to my size. She's tighter than I ever could have imagined. A perfect fit. I pull out slowly, watching as her pussy grips me, trying to suck me back in.

"You're mine, Lilith. You've always been mine. Say it."

"I'm yours. I'm yours!"

"Who do you belong to? Who's the only one dark enough to give you what you truly desire?"

"You, Wes. You."

"That's right. We belong together, little one. Nothing will ever change that."

I continue to thrust into her, her hips moving and meeting me stroke for stroke. Her pussy spasms around my shaft, her walls tightening and making it difficult to pull out, her body claiming me in the same way I'm claiming hers. I pull her legs up, forcing her to wrap them around my waist while I dig my fingers into the meaty flesh of her ass, lifting her bottom half off the ground. The position gets me deeper, pressing the tip of my dick to her cervix. I pound into her, giving her what I know her body needs. She screams every time I hit that barrier, tears streaming down her face, her black eye makeup dirtying her up even more. She's a mess, exactly what I wanted.

The wind howls and moans around us, the cold air pebbling

her nipples to stiff peaks behind the corset hiding them. I slow my pace, holding myself deep while rotating my hips, moving inside her in a languid dance. Reaching into the pocket of my jeans, I pull out my pocket knife. Her eyes widen as I flick it open, her mouth dropping open in a silent scream.

I place the flat side of the metal against her lips. "Shhhh. I've got you. I'll only ever give you pleasure. The pain only makes it that much better."

Her body relaxes but her pulse beats wildly in her neck. I love her fear. I lift the fabric of her tiny dress and cut, slicing down the center at her chest and using my hands to rip it open. Her breasts fall free of their confines, small, barely a handful, with little pink rosebuds pebbled and begging for my mouth. I lean forward, ready to feast on those sweet, perky little tits, and suck a nipple into my mouth.

Her moans are music to my ears as I suck. Pulling my hips back, I pull out to my tip and slam back in, picking up my pace. I release her nipple with a pop, bringing my blade back up to her sensitive flesh.

"I've been dying to taste you since you pricked your finger on that rose," I confess.

Delicately, I flick my knife over the top of her breast, cutting her just enough so that her blood pools across the nick. She flinches and gasps but doesn't fight me, never tells me no. With my eyes on her, I bury my cock in deep and drag the pad of my tongue across her blood, the taste of iron bursting on my tongue.

"Oh, god, Wes." Her moans fuel me, and I lock my mouth around it, sucking, pulling more from her, disappointed when the cut is too small. I repeat the process on the other side, only slightly deeper, completely feral and lost to the taste of her lifeblood. Her orgasm comes out of nowhere, her body shaking under me as she screams out, her nails digging in and dragging across my shoulder blades, breaking the skin. I knew she would love everything I'm capable of giving her. And this is only the beginning. This is only one piece.

I've had every bit of her now. There is no longer any part of her untouched by me. Satisfaction fills my chest. I take her mouth in a bruising kiss, our lips pressed tightly together as our teeth clash and tongues twist. When I release her, blood is smeared behind, and that's my undoing.

"I'm going to come inside you, Lilith, but you get to decide where." I thrust hard into her pussy as I grind out my next words, "Your cunt." I move my fingers through her swollen lips, pushing them in deep. "Your mouth." Moving them under us, rimming her little asshole. "Your ass? Tell daddy where you want to be filled up."

I pick up my pace, pulling all the way out and slamming back in. Her breasts bounce with the motion, her face twisted in a look of pure ecstasy. I love that I can make her feel this way, pull her free from all the expectations of her parents, life, and society. I know people—especially the people in our small town—will gasp and whisper, some will have issues. Our eighteen-year age gap will be enough to have people in her family clutching their delicate pearls. Add in the fact that she dated my son and we're a walking, talking recipe for an old-fashioned stoning. But I don't give a fuck. I'll protect her from it. Nothing is going to take her from me now.

"My mouth. I want to taste you," she finally answers, ending my torturous wait.

My eyes are heavily lidded, my vision no longer clear as I stare down at her. How could I ever deny her?

"You want daddy to fuck your face, Lilith? Is that what you want?"

I expect her to look at me with shame, unsure if my son left any damage from how he treated her, but her eyes light up in excitement, her body flushing with color as her pussy flutters around me. Yeah, that's exactly what she wants. I could let her have control, I could let her get on her knees, let her lead, but that's not what she asked for. Not what she needs. I pull my cock from her body and she whines at the loss. As she moves to sit up off the cold, dirty ground, my hand moves to the center of her chest, holding her down as I climb on top of her, straddling her waist.

"You want to be fucked? I'm going to fuck you," I say as I lean in and suck her lip into my mouth, dragging my teeth across it until I taste her blood. She whimpers before it turns into a moan. I do it again, biting a little deeper this time before repeating it to her top lip, leaving those plump pillows coated in her blood. I lean into her ear and whisper, "Because I don't want to accidentally kill you, tap my leg if it becomes too much."

I don't waste any more time talking, her mouth primed and ready to coat my cock in her blood and saliva. I didn't realize how badly I wanted this until this moment. My balls draw up and I have to talk myself off the ledge.

I move up her body, lining my cock up with her open, eager mouth before sinking into the warmth, her tongue caressing the underside of my dick, her mouth suctioning around me. I pull out, looking down my body to watch as her blood trails behind where her lips touched, admiring the red saliva rivulets dripping off her face. I smack her cheek with my cock before falling forward above her head, holding myself up with my hands. My eyes roll to the back of my head as I thrust back in, hitting the back of her throat. She gags beautifully, her hands shooting out and grabbing my ass, pulling me in deeper. How the fuck I lived thirty-eight years without this woman is a mystery, but I'll be damned if I live a second longer without her.

I fuck her mouth, just like she wanted, not holding back. One of her hands disappears for a moment between her legs before returning to me. Her hands grip the cheeks of my ass, spreading them open, and I can't help but tense. There's no way—

"Ohhh fuccccccck," I moan loudly as my hips stutter. Her wet, smooth fingers rim my asshole, pressing on the tight nerves there. She gathered up her fucking cum for lubrication. My smart, dirty little girl.

"Fucking. Do. It," I grit out.

One of her fingers breaches my hole, sinking in slowly, and the moment she reaches my prostate, rubbing the pad of her finger along that sweet spot inside me, I see fucking stars. My body stiffens, my cock hardening further, and I thrust three more times before I'm coming—lost to the most powerful orgasm of my entire life. My cum spills down her throat, filling her completely and overflowing, leaking out of the corners of her mouth. Her finger continues its motion on that spot inside me as the pleasure nearly makes me blackout.

I ease out of her mouth, and she slowly pulls her hand back, severing our physical connection. I drop down next to her, pulling her flush against me, wrapping her tightly in my arms as she gains control of her breathing, our hearts beating rapidly against each other.

"I'm not done with you yet. You still need to be punished."

"Punished?"

"You've been such a good girl for me, Lilith. But I need to teach you a lesson."

Her eyes widen as she starts to pull away from me, but I don't let her get far, grabbing her legs and dragging her back to me. I stand, picking her up in my arms like she weighs nothing at all. She fights me, pushing against me as I drop her onto the medical chair, forcing each of her limbs into the straps. She screams out, her nails scratching and digging into my flesh. Once she's completely restrained, I stand between her spread legs and look at her.

"You're a fucking divine goddess. I need to know that you learned a lesson tonight."

lily

I HAVE NO IDEA WHAT I DID AND FEAR FLOODS MY veins. Wes' eyes are still wild and crazed as he looks down at me. My body aches, my skin raw, bleeding from his bites and small cuts. My breath heaves as I wait for him to deliver my punishment. He walks away, bending over and pulling his belt from the loops on his jeans. My eyes dart everywhere, trying to understand. I'm strapped down on my back, my ass hanging off the end of the chair, spread open with all four of my limbs tied down.

"What are you doing with that?" I pant as he walks back to the chair, stopping between my spread legs.

"Making sure you understand."

He folds the belt in half, holding the buckle and the other end in his big palm. The cold leather drags across my sensitive flesh, from the base of my throat, down my torso, and over my swollen and sensitive center. I squirm against it. I close my eyes for a moment before I hear the small crack of the belt followed by a painful sting on my pussy. I scream, the pain ricocheting through my body. His fingers press inside me in slow motion, curving in deep and finding that blissful spot as his thumb rubs my clit and I moan. The pain and pleasure mingle into something so darkly depraved.

"You see how the two mix, my little demon?"

His hand pulls back and I feel the cold air before the belt slaps against my wet flesh. His hand returns, tenderly rubbing my sensitive pussy in all the right places.

I moan, thrashing my head side to side as an orgasm builds from somewhere deep inside me.

"The pain and the pleasure. This is what you need."

"Yesssssss!" I scream.

He pulls back again, the belt spanking my pussy two more times in rapid succession. Bloodcurdling screams escape me, but I don't sound like myself at all. I feel like a rabid, feral beast. His little demon.

His thick, huge cock replaces his fingers, driving in deep as his thumb works my clit. I'm crazed, my body on fire, and all I can do is give in completely. He's right. This is everything.

The pressure builds from deep in my belly, spreading through me in an orgasm so powerful I nearly black out. My body shakes as I don't hold anything back, tears weeping from my eyes. Wetness floods around us as liquid pulses out of me. I scream until my throat is hoarse.

"Oh fuck, yes, Lilith, that's it. Such a good little girl squirting for daddy."

He pounds into me, his thick cock hitting so deep inside me that I feel like I'm being ripped open. My body comes down from the high of my orgasm, going completely lax, my eyes drifting closed as he continues thrusting.

"I'm going to fill you up, baby. Paint your insides with my cum."

And he does, swelling inside me to the point of pain, jerking as he fills me with his cum.

He collapses on top of me, his head on my chest as we both work to steady our hearts and breaths. It's hard not to question if fate is real, if soulmates exist, when this man saw right through me. He gave me everything I wanted plus everything I didn't know I needed.

I'm irrevocably changed. All because of Wes Draven.

81

CHAPTER 17

WES

I LEAN FORWARD, KISSING HER LIPS GENTLY, PEPPERING her cheek and down the delicate space above her shoulders as lovingly as possible. Showing her with my body how deeply I feel for her.

Tonight went better than I could have hoped for. She was everything I knew she could be. The darkness hidden inside her played so well when coaxed out. I'm so proud of her. The trust it took to let go and experience this with me fills me with a sense of happiness and contentment I've never felt in my thirty-eight years.

Standing back, I unbuckle her ankles from the straps, lifting each leg and placing kisses along the reddened area. I repeat the process with her wrists before gathering her up in my arms and holding her naked, satiated body to mine.

"You're perfect, Lilith."

"I knew it was you," she admits through a whisper, her voice hoarse and cracking from her screams. "A part of me did at least. Or, I hoped it was you."

"I was hoping you would. You never seemed scared of me. Are you now?"

The lack of immediate response has me pulling back from her

slightly to peer down on her in my arms, trying to get a read on her facial expression.

"I'm not scared of you, Wes. I feel like you freed me. Did you mean everything you said?"

"Every word, little one."

"Good. I don't want to come back from this."

Her words fill me with satisfaction and relief. I love this woman. I couldn't bear it if she didn't want me in return.

"There is no going back from this. You're mine and I'm yours. Everything else be damned."

CHAPTER 18

lily

The sun shines into the bedroom, casting the light of a new day. A day that I wasn't ready for. If I could spend eternity in October I would. My mind swirls with the memories of Halloween, my brain a foggy haze of the events. Wes. My heart patters in my chest as it all flows back to me in waves of euphoric bliss. If my body didn't ache from head to toe I would convince myself it was all a dream. He's all I ever wanted for myself. Last night he brought me to a spare room in the asylum that had a backpack with a pair of leggings, a tank top, hoodie, and sneakers that he packed from my apartment while I was sleeping. He thought of everything so I could walk out of there with some decency after he shredded my costume. After we were dressed, he drove us home, claiming that my car had already been picked up and was sitting in front of my apartment. He really did plan out every detail.

I shift my sore body to the side, away from the harsh, unwanted sunlight, and face the man lying next to me. He's gorgeous. The upper half of his body is completely covered in ink, and I lightly trail my fingers over the intricate details of the art adorning his arm. He stirs in his sleep, reaching that same arm outward and wrapping around my back, pulling me flush against his front. His dick is awake, already hard and throbbing between us.

"Good morning," he mumbles, his voice raspy and deep with sleep and exhaustion. I run my fingers through his beard, loving the feel of it in my hand and through my fingers.

"Good morning, daddy," I purr, my core damp and craving more of him, even though everything aches. Pushing him to his back, I straddle his waist, lifting and grabbing his stiff cock to line up with my entrance and sink down. We both moan at the sensation of him filling me. I stay seated with him firmly planted inside me and rock my hips, riding him and chasing my pleasure. His hands rub up my thighs, gripping my hips and helping me move, his eyes roaming over all of me.

"I've waited for you for so long, Lilith. It feels like I've lived lifetimes while waiting."

His words trip up my heart, rapidly increasing my feelings for him, spreading like wildfire through my body. As if he read my expression and body language, his face lights up in a knowing smirk.

"I love you," he whispers, flipping us so that I'm on my back, and he's hovering over me. He grabs my face in his hands, kissing my lips sweetly. "I know you feel it, too, don't listen to your head, it's not too soon. We were meant to find each other. Even if you don't say it, I feel it."

"I love you, Wes Draven. I feel it. How could I not? I finally feel whole. I finally feel like me."

He drives into me, different from last night, slow and passionate as he devours my mouth with his. Together we climb that high, our bodies wrapped tightly around each other as we find our releases, tumbling off that cliff of bliss together.

After a long shower, where we took turns washing each other, I slipped on one of Wes' T-shirts and followed him downstairs to his kitchen where he made French toast. After finding the cabinet with cups, I pull out two, fill them with orange juice, and we sit next to each other at the table.

"I could get used to this," I confess as I take another bite of my French toast covered with real maple syrup.

"Good. You didn't think you were going anywhere, did you?" He winks and my heart flips again.

"You want me to stay . . . here?"

"Like I said, I feel like I've waited lifetimes for you. I don't want to wait any longer. Yes, I want you to stay. I never want you to leave." He reaches his hand out, tucking my hair behind my ear and dwarfing my cheek in his large palm.

The front door opens and shuts and I stiffen in my chair, my eyes widening, and I go to stand, to run. My heartbeat thunders, the rhythm loud in my ears. Wes places his hand over mine, immediately calming my nervous system. I look at him in question, unsure how this will go.

I look down at my plate, willing myself to disappear before the mortification sets in. Before I can summon dormant invisibility powers, Adam heads in our direction, his footsteps echoing off the hardwood floors.

"You're okay, my little one," Wes whispers as Adam waltzes into the room, stopping and gaping at us. I try not to wince, holding my own and preparing myself for whatever is to come.

"Wow! You're seriously fucking *her*?" Adam yells, his voice laced with venom. He moves his eyes to me. "What, couldn't get what you wanted from me so you seduced my *dad*? I told you she was fucking evil!"

"It's not—" I try to defend it, try to come up with words to defend myself, Wes, and this situation, but I'm interrupted.

"I'm not just fucking her, son. I'm in love with her."

My eyes go wide as a smile takes over my expression, my eyes blurring with tears, momentarily lost by the unexpectedness of his declaration to his son. I look toward Adam to gauge his reaction.

"Wow. So, I tell you my ex-girlfriend is a whore and you decide to fall in love with her. Cool, Dad, cool."

Wes stands so abruptly that the entire table shakes, orange juice spilling from the cups that were knocked over. He's on Adam so fast I don't think either of us saw it coming, his shirt balled in Wes' hand as he's pressed up against the wall. Wes cocks his fist back but holds it, the threat clearly there, Adam bracing for the blow we all thought was coming. Emotion is clogged in my throat, my heart pounding. I've never been defended before and my heart soars, but I desperately hate that I've come between father and son.

"I won't tell you again to watch how you fucking talk about her. You'll show her, and every other goddamn woman who walks this Earth the respect they deserve. If she wants to sleep with everyone in this fucking town she has that right without hearing judgment from the likes of you. If I hear one damn slur out of your fucking mouth again about Lily or any other female, I'll break your jaw, son or not. You hear me?"

I'm frozen, watching as Adam nods his head in agreement and is released from the grip Wes had on him. Adam turns on his feet and barrels out of the house. Wes returns to me and collapses into his chair, his elbows going to the table and his head falling into his hands. My heart hurts for him, and guilt starts to eat away at me.

"C'mere, please," he pleads.

Body on autopilot, I go to him, pushing him back into the chair so I can straddle his thighs to sit. I wrap my arms around his shoulders, pulling him into my chest for comfort. I can't imagine the internal fight he's having with himself.

"I'm so sorry, Wes."

"This is not your fault, little one. It's mine. I should have talked to him. I didn't expect him to come by."

"Do you want me to leave? I can . . ."

"Never. You're not leaving. Even if you try, it'll only excite me to hunt you down and bring you back home."

His words remind me of our game of cat and mouse last night

and fuel my imagination with all the possibilities of what our future will bring.

"Okay. But next time, you're hunting me in the woods."

He growls as he pulls me closer to him, burying his face into my chest.

I take a deep, settling breath, letting go of all the worry of what's to come, and choosing to focus on my new beginning. He may be double my age and my ex-boyfriend's dad, but he sees the real me, darkness and all, and loves me anyway. I usually hate November 1st, mourning that spooky season is behind me, but as I look at Wes, I know that it will be like Halloween any day we want it to be.

epilogue

SIX MONTHS LATER

"THANKS FOR MEETING ME."

"Glad you reached out, son. How are you?"

"I'm good, great actually. You?"

"I'm doing great, happy."

Adam looks around Bean Haven as if hoping for an escape, even though he's the one who reached out. He wipes his palms up and down his thighs nervously.

"You sure you're okay, Adam?"

"Eden's pregnant. We're, uh, having a little boy in June. I wanted you to know you're going to be a grandpa."

His news stuns me silent for a few moments.

"What happened to waiting until marriage and all that?"

"Yeah, well, shit happens that you can't fight sometimes. You know all about that, Dad. You going to judge me?"

I ignore his attempt at a jab and use of my decisions to justify his own.

"Are you happy?"

"Yeah, Dad, I'm happy."

"Then that's all that matters, Adam. I hope that someday you can see how happy I am and be happy for me, too."

"It's going to be weird, Dad. My ex-girlfriend is now legally my stepmom."

"I get it, but like you said, there are some things in life that you can't fight. I never could have stayed away from her, Adam, and she feels the same. It wasn't done maliciously."

"Yeah, I know. Doesn't mean I want to talk about it."

"I'm happy for you. Congratulations on the baby. I hope that we can move forward as a family someday."

"Yeah, I want to work toward that."

We finish our coffees and I leave Bean Haven to head home to my wife as the sun is setting. We have plans, and I know she'll be anticipating me. I walk up to the tree line behind our house, acres of woods on our property left untouched for the privacy it brings. I stretch my neck from side to side, breathing in deeply for any sign of my little one. Before I can take a step out of the clearing and into the forest, clouds open up and rain starts to pour down. My lips turn up in a twisted smile at the thought of my little she-demon's soaking wet, trembling body as she races through the woods in the rain. I take a deep breath before starting my hunt.

Ready or not, here I come.

thank you for reading!

LOVED WES & LILY'S STORY?

Please consider leaving a review! As an indie author, reviews are so important! Thank you so much for your support.

Not ready to leave Aspen Ridge? Check out the full series now and meet the Hayes family as they each find love.

Aspen Ridge Series

Unravel Me

Crave Me

Love Me

Wreck Me

Complete Me

Aspen Ridge Holiday Novellas

Ready or Not

Sweet Girl

Daddy Issues

acknowledgments

Happy Halloween! Thank you for reading. I hope you enjoyed Wes and Lily's story as much as I enjoyed writing it. October is my favorite month and I look forward to Halloween all year long. I knew I wanted to write a dark romance around our mysterious Aspen Ridge PI and it turned out better than I could have imagined.

Michael,

Thank you for your support while I juggled writing not one but two freaking books at the same time. You are a saint for picking up my slack and encouraging me to keep going. Thank you for loving all of me, my dark side included.

Madalyn P.,

I hope I did this book justice. I tried to include all of our favorites. Someday we'll be able to sit together during spooky season and read all of the dark primal play books together. Until then, I hope you enjoyed this one, my little demon. I love you.

My editor and friend, Katie,

Thank you for supporting my crazy idea to write a novella while working against a deadline for Crave Me. I couldn't have done this without your support and encouragement. I finally got to work through my need to write a dark romance and while I didn't get to stuff a dead body in a whiskey barrel, I'm pretty proud of this one. Working with you is a dream and I'm so thankful to have you by my side while we bring these stories to life. I love you!!

My amazing PA, Meighan,

I would be a hot mess without you. Thank you for keeping my shit together so I can focus on writing and getting lost in these stories I dream up. You work so hard to make me look good and you take care of so much. Thank you for choosing to be by my side. I love you!

My alpha readers, Lauren and Laura,

I couldn't (and wouldn't) do this without you two in document with me. You constantly adapt to my insane writing process, you keep me on track, grounded, focused, and push me to grow as a writer. I'm so thankful for your love of Aspen Ridge and seeing each of these characters' stories told. That last weekend was a long one before I sent this off but you two were saints helping me make sure it was ready for edits. Thank you for your time, and your work in every area of this book's creation. But most of all, thank you for loving me. I love you both an insane amount.

Danielle and Nouha,

Thank you for keeping all of my author secrets when I'm too excited to keep them to myself. You both have known about this project since the beginning and it was the only thing keeping me from screaming about it to anyone who would listen. Each of us were drowning in writing and edits this summer and I'm so proud of us for surviving and kicking ass!!

Dani, thank you for the endless pep talks and vent sessions to keep me in check and focused. It was exactly what I needed. I love you both!

Rebeca, Morgan, & Scott,

Thank you for taking the time to read early drafts of this book and giving me such helpful feedback. I am forever grateful for your time and support.

My harlots,

Each of you means the world to me. Your support, hype, enthusiasm and love for my books blows me away. I'm so thankful to have you all on this journey with me!

To every ARC reader, bookstagrammer, reviewer, and blogger,

Thank you for reading. Every post, review, and tag mean the world to me. I'm obsessed with all of your edits, and the creative ways you all bring my characters to life. Thank you for your support!

To every reader,

YOU are making my dreams come true. Thank you for reading!

about the author

Author, wife, mother, lover of reading, overcast skies, chilly
weather, and hockey.

A romantic at heart, Jenn has always been a lover of books and is
constantly dreaming up heart-wrenching stories that will have you
reaching for tissues and make you blush.

When Jenn's not writing, she can be found reading a spicy
romance novel, watching scary movies, and enjoying her quiet life
in New England, living out her real-life romance story.

Follow along for updates on new releases and book news.

www.jennplummer.com
Instagram @authorjennplummer
Goodreads @jennplummer
Amazon @jennplummer
Threads @authorjennplummer

unravel me

CHAPTER ONE IVY

"That stupid motherfucker!"

"I'll drink to that."

Picking up my next shot of tequila, I gently knock it against my best friend's before tossing it back. Wincing, I reach for the lime and press it between my lips, sucking the crisp tartness into my mouth.

"How is this my life? Honestly, Zoe, what the fuck am I going to do now? I can't afford rent in Seattle on my own." My voice leaks with desperation and I cringe. I need to be stronger than this if I'm going to keep it together.

Today I walked in on my semi-long-term boyfriend railing the bikini barista from the coffee stand down the street, doggy style, in our bed. As if that wasn't bad enough, the asshole glared at me like *I* had done something wrong. He didn't look shocked that I had come home early, no, his face reddened in anger and frustration that his orgasm was interrupted. You can't make this shit up. As the severity of my situation sinks in, I drop my forehead down on the cold bar top.

The worst part? Because trust me, it gets worse. Not only is it his apartment that I was living in, but the restaurant I'm the sous chef for? His parents own it.

Yep. Let that settle in. Luckily my natural flight response kicked in—something I've become somewhat of a pro at—and I ran off to Zoe's apartment to figure things out and process the dumpster fire that has become my life.

The alternative would have been to bash his head in with a table lamp, which was a thought that crossed my mind while watching him rut into the rando. Even though I'm fairly sure that'd be considered a crime of passion, I couldn't take my chances. So, here I am sitting at a bar in Downtown Seattle with my best friend, slinging back shots like we're twenty-one again. It's this or jail time. I may project that I'm tough and can handle a whole hell of a lot, but that's all a carefully built façade, and I know I'm not cut out for jail.

"Well. I was thinking . . ."

"That's never a good thing for me, Zo . . ."

"Don't kill me, but, you could always move back home? Like, to Aspen Ridge. You've got your parents' house just sitting there empty," she suggests sheepishly.

"Ha. You're kidding, right? I'd rather take my chances on the street. I have no interest in ever facing the ghosts that fill that house or live in that town."

"Ivy. Listen. I get it. I know your heart and I hear you."

I go to interrupt, and she puts her hands up to stop me.

"I know what you're going to say. It's the memories. It's what the house represents. I get it, babe. I do. But it's an entire house just sitting there. You sell that fucker and your situation would change drastically. I don't want you to move for any amount of time, but damn. If it was me, I'd be pouncing all over that opportunity. How many people get left a paid-off house for fuck's sake?"

I'm not hearing any of it. My parents got pregnant with me when my mom was nineteen and my dad was thirty-four. It was a huge scandal in town and caused serious heartache for the grandparents I never had the chance to meet. They cut my mom off when she chose my dad, completely ashamed of her decisions and unwilling to support her. Not long after, they moved out of state, and I've never had contact with them.

When I was a little girl, my mom used to tell me her dreams of becoming a writer who traveled all over the world and wrote about her experiences. She gave up the life she had dreamed for herself to be with my dad because she believed in the fairytale of it all, believed in him and his pretty words.

My childhood was spent being told how important it was for me to grow up and leave Aspen Ridge, to go into the world on my own and make something of myself. My mom was a dreamer and wanted to see me live the life she never got to. As I got older I watched her wither away, losing her dreams and the love she traded them for.

Once upon a time she happily changed the course of her life to be with my dad. She was in love. But he was rarely home, and when he was, I never saw them be affectionate with one another, never saw my dad show her love or support. He feigned indifference to both of us. Her heartbreak became more and more evident as the years passed and she sank further into depression. I thought that my parents had a fairytale love story when I was little, but the hard truth of it was that my father preyed on and exploited my mother and her naivety. She may have loved him, but he just wanted to own her. His something young and pretty that he kept at home, locked in her gilded cage. She never had the opportunity to build her own life. She was simply embedded into his already existing one.

My parents were killed in a car accident fifteen months ago and my mom never left Washington. While I work hard to keep the promises I made to my mother—that I would leave Aspen Ridge and create a life on my own—it's hard not to ask myself if this is what *I* really wanted to begin with.

After all, I was happy in Aspen Ridge . . . at one point.

"It's my dad's house, Zo. I don't want anything from him. He's given me enough and I have the therapy bills to prove it. End of discussion."

"Okay, okay, point made. You know you can couch surf at my place for as long as you need, we'll make it work until you're on your feet again."

"I love you for it." I drop my head back and take a deep inhale. "Why's it so difficult to not stick your dick in things that you shouldn't? Is monogamy really that hard?"

"Seeing as how I don't have a dick, I'm really not sure. Brooks is an asshole, Ivy. But tonight we're going to forget about that cheating fuckface and party like the confident, gorgeous, badass women we are. We'll face this shitstorm tomorrow."

I give her a halfhearted smile. I loathe going out. It's never been my scene. I'm much more a "grab a beer and sit on the bed of a truck and watch a bonfire" kinda girl. But I love her for trying.

"Can't we go back to your place, order a pizza, and binge on some trashy tv?"

"Uh. No. You need to get out and be out of your head."

"You're the worst."

"But you love me." She waves the bartender down, who she's been checking out since we got here.

"Hey, what can I get you?"

"Hmm. I'm in the mood for a screaming orgasm if you can manage," she says with a flirty wink.

The bartender's eyebrows shoot to his forehead at her bluntness, and I let loose a nervous laugh.

"Don't mind her. She's absolutely insane. She means the shot, not her. Vodka, Kahlua, Irish cream, and amaretto, I think." Quickly trying to recall her go-to shot.

As he walks down the bar away from us, she smacks me on the arm.

"You're such a buzzkill."

"We're nursing my shitty life tonight, just like you said, not hooking up with bartenders, no matter how hot they are."

"Hey, there's an idea. You could always pick up some bartending shifts for extra cash. That's an option!"

I groan. Loudly.

"I can't go back to bartending, Zo, c'mon. That would be like going backward in my career. Actually, it is going backward in my career. Chef by day, bartender by night. No thanks. Plus, the men are such pigs."

Add bartending to the list of things I'd rather not be doing. The tips were incredible at the restaurant I used to work at, but it was a taxing job in an environment that made me want to crawl out of my skin.

"It's 'cause you're such a smoke show, babe. They can't help but want a piece of you."

"You keep thinking that," I say, rolling my eyes at her.

"If I didn't think it'd ruin our relationship, I'd be trying to get a lick for myself."

I toss my head back in a deep laugh.

When I say my best friend is crazy, I mean it. Her audacity knows no bounds. She is the quintessential life of the party. We met in California during our college days while working at the same bar. When I wanted to move back to Washington, she was down to stick with me. Our relationship was that insta-connection kind of friendship. We're the epitome of opposites attract, though, and it's obnoxiously obvious in most situations.

She has gorgeous ice-blonde hair that she keeps in a stylish bob, whereas mine is midnight-black and down to my waist. She's loud, where I'm more quiet. She's a vivacious extrovert, while I'm a textbook introvert. My circle contains her. If it wasn't for her forcing me around others, I would be at home reading. She has made my life immensely better since she came into it and as cliché as it may be, I'd be lost without her. Craziness and all. She's my ride or die.

My phone goes off for the tenth time in the last thirty minutes. Pulling it out of my purse, I slide it across the bar in Zoe's direction, laying my forehead back on the bar top with a groan.

"Your turn. It's him again, isn't it?"

Zoe picks up my phone and glances over the texts before turning it to face me so I can read them.

"Man, he went from pompous dickwad to full-on maniacal overlord in the span of an hour. Fuck, Ivy."

I read over the slew of texts that get progressively more intense.

Brooks: We need to talk about this. Come home and we will get through it.

Brooks: Ivy. You don't want to do this.

Brooks: Answer your goddamn phone. I swear to fucking God Ivy don't ignore me.

I push the phone back to her, unable to focus on any of it. I can't let this get to me.

"Just put it away. Turn it off. Throw it out the fucking window for all I care. He's just pissed he was caught." I sit up and twist my hands together in my lap before shaking them out at my sides, doing my best to control my breathing. This will not get under my skin. The last thing I need today is a panic attack in the middle of a bar.

"C'mon then, my girl, let's get you drunk and have some fun!"

We spend the next two hours sipping on drinks and dancing on the dance floor. Zoe does everything she can to help me forget the day and enjoy the moment, but my mind continues to flood with anxiety over how to move forward.

We take an Uber back to Zoe's studio apartment around midnight and I fall onto her couch to hopefully get some sleep. Zoe's suggestion that I move back home has been on constant repeat throughout the night. That damn house really is just sitting there. I lay awake in the dark room, doing my best to work through every scenario. I have some savings that can get me through for a while, but not if I want to stay in Seattle. With the cost of rent, I would plow through it too quickly. But maybe if I moved back to Aspen Ridge temporarily and sold my parents' house, this could set up my life and give me the boost I desperately need. As I envision what it would be like to be back in my hometown for the first time in ten years, my mind drifts to thoughts of the boy whose heart I shattered by leaving. The boy who loved me so fiercely. Who planned our life together.

And I ran. Hard and fast and never looked back.

Until now.